The Time Machine
Homo Sapiens Version

I0672589

Monarch Srivastava

DIAMOND BOOKS

www.diamondbook.in

© Author

Publisher : **Diamond Pocket Books (P) Ltd.**
X-30, Okhla Industrial Area, Phase-II
New Delhi-110020
Phone : 011-40712200
E-mail : sales@dpb.in
Website : www.diamondbook.in

The Time Machine : Homo Sapiens Version
Author – Monarch Srivastava

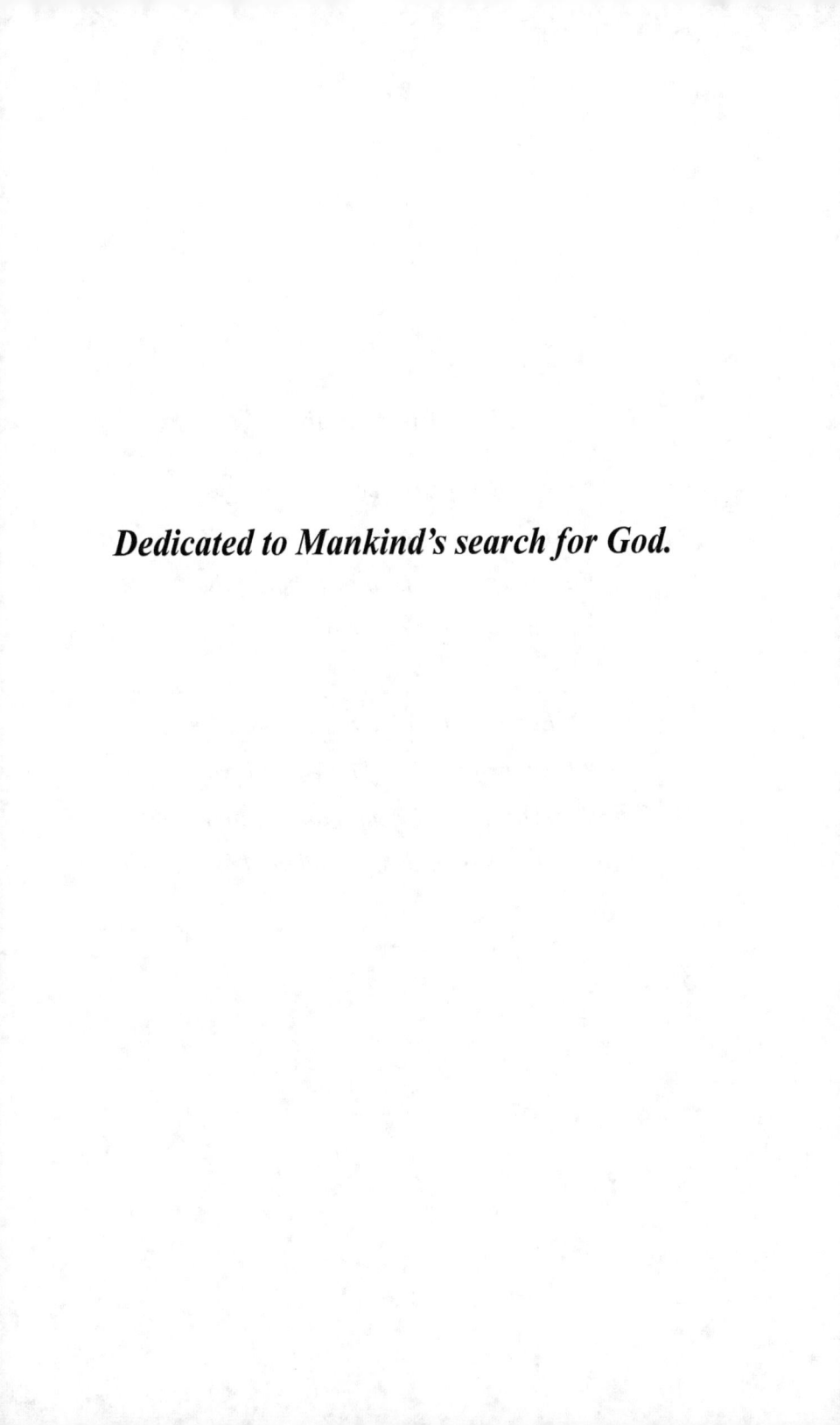

Dedicated to Mankind's search for God.

The First Adam

From ages past there came a cry:
"I am 'Adam' from heav'n on high.
What purpose, this, that I should live,
And carry in all men to give?

"Of Earth and Moon and stars above,
Of poor and rich, of hate and love.
Through height and breadth and depth below,
To oceans, mountains, friend, and foe! ...

Acknowledgement

I acknowledge you all who are going to read this manuscript in order to look for our almighty.

My tireless literary is filled with an extreme motivation filled by my father Mr. Anil Srivastava who imputed his notion for mankind, unknowingly in my brain.

I would also like to thank Mrs. Patricia Peterson, senior manager at Canadian Imperial bank, who supported me throughout the creation of this writing.

This book was impossible to create without the inspiration from my mom Mrs. Sheela Srivastava and my lovely sister Monalisa. Both of them were a great support throughout this manuscript.

I want to thank Jayesh Sathwara and Mitpal Singh Chauhan, who have heard my mankind story one hundred million times while I was writing it. I actually wanted to have a second set of eyes at my work so their help and support is graciously appreciated.

At last but not the least, I would like to thank my brother Amritesh Srivastava, who has offered his unconditional support, guidance and motivation throughout the times and without his help this book would never have reached in your hand.

Author's Note

The twenty-first century most advanced, innovative, and intelligent species in all kinds of life on our planet Earth, are us, "The Homo Sapiens." Yes, you, I, and every living human being on this powered surface.

Maybe some people know, and some don't about our incredibly special life and time span. But those who are unknown to this, would get to know eventually, when they cross their younger age.

Earth is a home for humans and millions of other living creatures. Some live close to us and some hide from us and live in jungles, oceans, mountains, and deserts. But, "humans" are the superior among all other species and sovereign to this wonderful planet.

Right now, we are living in a society where our lives are too complex to understand. After spending a few years at school, we work towards the source of income.

To earn it, we will have to pay some precious time in our lives. The more time we give away the wealthier we become. Then we get married, have children, grandchildren, and die. These popular life-cycle phases are very common among humans.

Other than family and friends, human life is also surrounded by different other deep worlds like entertainment, education, economy, government, and many more. Financial and stock markets are the most complicated and deepest ones. It's easy enough to get lost in one of these worlds.

If you are going to talk about today's life complexities, we will not be able to finish them even for decades. But, why are we living our lives? What is the purpose? If there is any purpose, why just a hundred years to everyone?

We're all given the same time to live our lives, but by the time we understand our time limit, it certainly has wasted heavy time prior to that point. Then we think, "Now it's time to settle down, with a family, then they get married, have children, grandchildren, and similarly die."

The truth is, they never had a chance to understand their life time management. We always think, wish we could go back in time and do some major changes, which could change our present life scenario.

Well, physics demonstrates that time can be stretched, shrunk, and go forward, but no human has found how to go backwards.

I have developed this virtual time machine which would take us in the past and proclaim a well-mannered future by ourselves. It will also explain about our special human life and its short duration of "The Hundred Years".

Preface

Welcome to this manufactured virtual time machine. Biologically and in real, there is no difference in your (reader) and writer's intelligence or mind. It is something our human body structure and day to day social, economic, and technological development made us humans "Homo Sapiens".

There were many story books written in the past in reference of a king, person, hero, leader, group, nation, or religion. Every story has something we can connect ourselves to motivate with somebody else's victory. But this story book is going to uncover you as a hero and your unprecedented victory for the entire humankind. We are going to discover who we are, and where did we come from? And, are we developed enough yet to know these questions with evidence?

This writing would demonstrate, the most important aspects of human life, age, caliber, and origination. We will go in different time and places in the past/future and understand more about us. All the events are true; however, dates and times are approximated.

Prelude

It's November 4, 2015 and Justin Pierre James Trudeau and his cabinet ministers are going to swear for the 42nd Canadian Parliament today.

For the good deed of people, the 'Liberal party' had really made a difference while partition from the United States of America in 1867 A.D., George Brown, and the other legends from this group, fought for humanity and the basic human rights at this time.

Mr. Trudeau is representing a political party which was started when Canada was just being born. The Liberal party has lost its trust and promises in the past few years. While the party was going through with major breakdowns, the Conservative party, and the New Democratic Party, came into the play. They had created another kind of picture among civilians.

People have already given their love and support to Justin Trudeau in the 2015 Federal elections. As a young, educated employee, Prime Minister Trudeau is just not going to keep providing the basic human rights, but taking some extra steps to save humanity from the calamity change as global warming.

Canada is one of the safest places where global warming still hasn't stamped its presence yet. Where other countries are facing terrific global warming effects, Canadians feel safer today.

The Canadian government is working too hard to understand our unknown reality. The reality, which is directly related to humans, will decide our future on Earth. There are many countries which have separated their funding for innovations and explorations.

In 2020 A.D., due to the global warming effect, many countries are now participating to save our planet, and spending billions of dollars on these projects.

Canada is one of those countries who are involved in many exploration projects today. The Canadian government also thinks that the Earth will not be a habitant place forever, as the Sun is growing bigger, day by day. Deadly solar flares and the global warming effect will make our future generations helpless.

Government officials have now decided to go one step ahead and lead the world to save our planet. This year, the government has presented an extra budget in the assembly for many exploration projects which could help people all over the world.

The government predicts a complete ice melt on our planet by the end of the 21st century. The way the arctic cap and Greenland's ice are melting, the ocean level has risen very high. This extra water has been covering the land mass from the last few hundred thousand years since the ice age.

About 19 thousand years ago, the ocean level was about 121 meters below than the present level. There was drastic climate change in the last hundred years, especially after 1933. The climate and geological change were taking place because of human greed becoming the most powerful and iconic human on Earth, and beyond.

This increased water has wiped out many manufactured coastal cities in the past and will also create damage in the future. This process of extra water on the land doesn't happen overnight because ice melts slowly over the years, and people back up little by little from the coastal line to the middle part of the land.

Continuous use of natural resources such as coal, gas, and oil, result in huge carbon emissions, which are drastically heating up the planet's atmosphere.

To stop carbon emissions and start a new electric life, the government wants to create a "manual" for people all over the world so that they can understand more about humans and the atmosphere to contribute their share for future human races.

The government really thinks that the Time Machine project will help us to understand about human age and its importance. Fleming College is the obvious institution for this project, as they have been researching on time travel for almost a decade. With the help of the Canadian Space Agency (CSA), Fleming College's hard work is now touching the finishing line with a new Time Machine project.

To create a 'manual' for the public understanding of humans, the government is using this time machine for more data. The technology they are using in this machine is called 'Atom Transportation System'.

In this machine, technology will take a high resolution 'Video camera' to a different dimension. This process will break this camera into millions of subatomic parts and send it to a different time and place. They have created some sort of gravity and sound waves attached to this camera that takes them in different time and place without even breaking the signal.

Summer, 2020
Place: Fleming College, Ontario, Canada.
Time: 8:45 a.m.

Olivia: Good morning, Mr. Chairman! I hope you have had a nice trip to Moscow.

Chair: Good morning, Professor! The trip was fantastic! Trust me, I was physically in Moscow, but my mind was here in our research facility. I was curious to know about our Time Machine project which the government has recently assigned us.

Olivia: Mr. Chairman! As you know, we have the best engineers and research team in the world. I am pleased to say that, with the help of my brilliant colleagues, we have completed, and are ready for the time travel in next 20 days.

Chair: Well done, Professor! But what about the safety procedures? We don't want anybody's life at risk.

Olivia: Mr. Chairman! The unique thing in our project is technology. Under 'Atom Transportation System,' we transport atoms in a fraction of a second and protect any structure in its actual shape. We have safely done these trials multiple times in the past for a few months.

Chair: This is fantastic, Professor! I want you to take the best student with you as your assistant. He will accompany you to observe and record your time travel trip. I also want you to submit a detailed thesis after the completion of your journey for the University record. By the way, when are you leaving for Cambridge Bay?

Olivia: We are leaving on the thirtieth of this month.

Chair: Good luck, Professor! Who is going from the CSA?

Olivia: Mr. Chairman, it's my pleasure to represent our college to help humanity and astrophysicist Mr. Jimmy Ludrasky is going to represent the Canadian Space Agency at Cambridge Bay. There would be one more representative from the government official's, but we don't know about them yet. We will meet them directly at Cambridge Bay.

Chair: Good luck, Professor!

20 days later

Place: James Armstrong Richardson Airport

Saria: I just wanted to let you know that I love you so much and will wait for you until the last breath of my life. I know that we have gone through some bad times, but I won't sell drugs any more. Maybe we could elope somewhere and make our own dream world.

Xing: Shh! Stop saying that. I am in the government service now. I cannot support you with your drugs anymore. You must understand, my love, this wouldn't take you anywhere, but to the end of life, and I still want to live this life with you. Look at me, I have studied hard and the university has selected me to record and observe the world's biggest help for humanity.

Saira: I understand; we are not kids anymore, but you know it's not easy to get out of this addiction.

Xing: Listen to me, love, I am coming back, and we'll leave this................country and go far away.

Olivia: (waving hand in the airport lobby from a distance) Xing, come on, hurry up!

Xing: Coming! I've got to go, my love! I will come back soon. Running towards Olivia, he gives her an ambiguous smile.

Olivia: Who was she? Your girlfriend?

Xing: Yes, Professor! We love each other too much and will be together again once we complete this Time Machine project.

Olivia: Indeed! You will. Are you ready for the flight to Cambridge Bay?

Xing: Yes, Professor! I am excited.

Time: A day earlier at 3:00 p.m.
Place: Adam Research Facility (ARF), Cambridge Bay, Canada
    (Helicopter sounds while Daphne introduces herself to Richard, the caretaker of the facility.)

Daphne: Hi! I'm Daphne Stevenson and the representative from the government. This is my ID. Also, meet Zeus, he is my assistant for shooting videos for government records.

Richard: Welcome to Cambridge Bay! The facility is a little far from here, so we'll need to ride through the town up in the hills.

Zeus: Why's everybody staring at us? (on the way back to facility)

Richard: The local people have never experienced this kind of government involvement in this little isolated town. Survival is not easy here. The community around here is mostly involved in fishing, and people make their living out of it. They live their life here in peace, which you guys are disrupting.

Daphne: To be honest, I'm simply here to record everything as my appointment for this job from the government. I don't have any personal attachment with this project.

Richard: That's good to hear. Well, we're here now. This glass facility was made twenty years ago for some Alien project but vanished in political chaos.

Your rooms are upstairs. The other teams are on their way and will meet you in "Adam's Hall" at 10:00 a.m. You may go now. The dining and kitchen rooms are next to the living area.

Daphne: Thank you! Zeus! Get your stuff and put it upstairs.

Time: 10:00 a.m. Next day

Place: Adam's Hall

Olivia: Our journey onward is very special, as our goal is to understand the question as to who we are as humans today. Where did we come from? And, why are we surviving on this planet for a limited time? Why do humans live only a hundred years, whether you are a leader, king, or a freedom fighter? Nor does it matter whether you're a pop singer, dancer, or a Hollywood icon. It doesn't even matter if you're Gautama Buddha, Moses, or any other religious leader. Everybody has the same life coupon of the 'Hundred Years'. It's a harsh truth but if you are in human shape, you must follow the same "nature rule" during your life span.

In the 21st century A.D., our life structure is entirely different from all the other previous life years. Things were completely different even before our birth. This change of our society made us modern. These changes include technology, climate, human needs and wants, biology, and there may also be some innovation which has changed our lifestyle completely.

The best example in 2018 A.D. is a smart phone device. A generation ago, people were ancient to cell phones, and now it has become an important bond of relation. Human society has been developing and changing on an everyday basis. These changes include human brain development (biology), technological changes, political changes, and environmental changes like global warming, or even deadly solar flares. This is true that our life has been changing because of our creative intelligence and curiosity but it is also affected by some external powers.

So, to understand about external hazards, we will travel back to some catastrophic natural or global events, and for internal hazards, we will travel back to some special people. These people aren't with us anymore, but their sayings, speeches, and writings have completely changed the pattern of human life. Again, we all are here in the service of the people of Canada and the government has given us an opportunity to help the entire humankind. When our video camera travels in another time, the sight will show up on this black screen.

We are honoured to have Mr. Jimmy Ludrasky from the Canadian Space Agency. I will observe the sights and narrate the story of the Time Machine manual. Daphne and her assistant will make their own videography records for the government database.

Jimmy: Thank you, Professor Mercer! I would like to introduce my metallic/robotic assistant, "BERT". He's been programmed to handle this Time Machine and will help us in this project.

BERT: Hello everyone! The following destinations contain parts to be assembled. It's up to the serious traveler to follow the instructions, put the destinations and clues together, plug it in, and take off on the deepest journey of humankind.

Xing: Right on!

Contents

Nuclear energy atomic bomb, Book of the dead, Cloning & God's avatar, Future irrelevance of humans, technology AI, Homo Pyrus

Destination A
Ancient Civilizations

BERT: Main engine starts. Passenger! Please fasten your seatbelt.

Jimmy: Human psychedelic power of superiority have its way through cruelty, its nature that how he had changed from a naked human to a greedy civilian.

Base : Station I

Time : 13 Years 5 Months 3 days

Type : Past

Speed: (Speed of Light) X 12.34

Place : Iraq

Olivia: Sixteen days have already gone, and the invasion of Iraq is still in hot news today and will go in the history books right after few days. Today is April 3rd, 2003 and the chaotic environment being everywhere.

Innocent civilians are dying, and precious natural oil wells are turning into brutal wildfire. We are in the middle of battlefield here, camouflaging all U.S tanks and fighter aircrafts full of skies.

Have a look at those precious antiques which are burning and looting by local thieves at the National Museum of Iraq. Some antiques and pieces belong to our first human civilization on our planet. It could be anything. Maybe our first coin, first bowl or any other important writing message document crafted by our ancestors several thousand years ago. This is the perfect time for looters as Baghdadian guards are busy in protecting their leaders and powerful ministers while U.S. forces are busy in protecting ministry of oil.

Civilians are terrified in this bloodshed. Many of them are dreaming for their freedom from a cruel monopolist leader, Saddam Husain, who supports crime and terrorism. Others are confused on how they should react for their motherland when externals are roaming around with the most advanced weapons and armed forces.

A hundred and sixty-thousand troops, including the U.S., U.K., Australia, and Poland are fighting in a foreign country when in January 2003, the CBS poll has presented a result of 63% majority against it, and wanted Bush to find a diplomatic solution, rather than invading a country.

Government of France, Germany and New Zealand are having a cup of tea in their home countries and are totally standing back on this matter after a long, live friendship with U.S.

Xing: But, what happened? Why did humans want to turn one of the world's largest oil reserve into burning gases?

Olivia: U.S. President, George W. Bush and U.K. Prime minister, Tony Blair allies together and claims this is for a good fate of Iraqis by giving them freedom from its cruel anarchy. We can certainly refer today's newspaper for different views on this unjustifiable intervention. Millions of people protested this war in Rome and other parts of the world.

Some of their opinions have a sound of revenge of nine eleven, which happened a couple of years ago in 2001. It was an extremely unfortunate incident which made humankind think twice about humanity. The twenty-first century has brought many disasters right in the beginning of the first few years. Nine-eleven in 2001, Iraq war in 2003, and the subprime crisis in 2008 A.D. made thousands of people die in terrorism and greed.

Jimmy: Historically, Iraq's land is not new to this kind of disaster. This land's been shadowed by several wars, events, entertainments, and kings' marches with blades and spears in the past. Archeologists have been researching from centuries about our previous civilizations and some extent of our true ancestors.

As humans' step into the future, they would have multiples of theories, writings, and archeological evidences. These theories paint a picture as to who we are as humans and where did we come from?

Among all these theories around the globe, most of the world's population are affected by three major theories:

• Human Evolution from Apes - DNA based science evidence
• Evolution from Adam & Eve - Monotheist
• Hindu Gods creation - Brahma, Vishnu, and Mahesh as (Manu)

Human evolution from apes is a scientific DNA proven evidence as to how we evolved from time to time in different breeds in our mammal pyramid, which cannot be ignored.

We cannot ignore Hindu (Sanatan) scriptures either as they are the oldest written scriptures and messages around the globe. These historic scriptures were written even long before Jesus and Buddha.

It's unfortunate, but in the 20th & 21st century A.D., Hindu themselves call these scriptures as 'Mythology' instead of a message from our great ancestors. Today, these scriptures are testifying and verifying by modern scientists with curiosity for an underlying treasure of human origination.

We have also heard about monotheism, which is the Adam & Eve story, that they were the first humans on our planet, as well as our first ancestors. Let's just imagine for a minute, if that is a true story but, where did they come from? Look at your body structure now, do you really think it is possible to give this kind of complex body structure with a magic wand?

Monotheists including Jewish, Christians, and Muslims ignore science evolution from apes and at the same way, science ignores Adam & Eve evolution. Science justifies, "It cannot be possible that Adam & Eve were the first humans on our planet, but it could be possible that they were the finest piece of our distant ancestors who started their lives hundreds of thousands of years prior to their existence."

With archeological evidences, about 3,25,000 years old, Homo Sapiens' skeletons have been found in Morocco recently. This proves that Adam and Eve are at least evolved 300,000 years ago.

Humans have invented writing about 6000 thousand years ago with the help of symbols, letters, and drawings. So, how could anyone know about the complete channels of hundreds, or thousands of years, of human generations?

Why is everybody ignoring each other? Who is right and who is wrong? Only one of them could be right or they are all right and connected to each other.

Jimmy: It was become clear that humans started their lives on a handful of places about 14,000 B.C. This is the very first time when sapiens started strengthening their roots to the society. This golden age of Homo Sapiens' breed brought a new revolution to a genetic life.

People, those who were easy meal for wild animals, reflected as a hunter and a killing machine. Wild animals started getting away from the flock of humans.

These humans started living together so that they can protect themselves in numbers. This protection of love as human for another human spread across the world in no time and later this loving habit created small, big, and eventually, the biggest groups around the world.

There were few civilizations flourished on our planet which ended due to the catastrophic effect of global warming. In the beginning, few human groups had started living together around the coastal areas. They had created some of the greatest kingdoms at the shore.

But again, due to global warming, ice on the arctic cap started melting so quickly that all these cities at the coast drained deep down in the ocean. There were many marine evidences found from these underwater cities.

Scientists have been creating a simulation that how much land was covered after this ice melt. The government was shocked when they found that the ocean has already covered about 90 miles of the land area under water. After thousands of years as experienced humans, they now have understood the drawback of a coastal disaster, building their kingdoms in the middle of the land somewhere.

This is identical to any other ice melt. Take an ice cube and put it under sunlight. You will see it melts first and then evaporates in the atmosphere. In the same way the Arctic and Greenland ice are melting first, and eventually evaporating as well.

The only thing which buys us some time is to not let this life– giving water in the ozone and atmosphere evaporate. But it's going to be more humid and a worse atmosphere in the greenhouse gas effect.

Olivia: But this is the worst-case scenario. Humans will be complete electric and will call as 'Type I' civilization instead of 'Type 0' soon.

BERT: Time one-minute remaining to Jericho City.

Olivia: There were four different spots back in time from where these extraordinary humans started their 'journey of life' one after another.

Neolithic period civilization, Mesopotamia, Egypt, and the Indus Valley civilization were the oldest with archeological evidences and proof so far. Modern humans call these groups as 'cradles of civilization'.

People were still living in smaller groups on some other places on our planet, like in the Jungle of America, Southern India, Yellow river, China, but they weren't big enough to call as a civilization. Humans actually had evolved, all around the Earth, but they were living isolated in very small groups. A civilization includes an entire city and economy run by few people or leaders in that particular group.

Base   : Station II

Time : 14,000 BC

Type : Past

Speed: (Speed of Light) X 12.34

Place : Levant - Jericho City

Olivia: In the Neolithic period, Levant (today Jericho) was the first Palestinian City near the Jordan River in the middle of the Mediterranean ocean and the Dead Sea. It was the first place when people got together and started living as a community. These Natufian people lived by hunting and gathering.

Jericho was perished in northern Israel with some hard-working people. The Natufian culture existed mainly in 12,500 BC, a region in the Eastern Mediterranean.

Humans were being tired of getting isolated; failing against wild animals, where they started building the very first Neolithic settlements (house) of the region, which may have been the earliest in the entire world.

Jimmy: In 2008 A.D., archeologists have found a 12,000-year-old grave of a Natufian female which was well preserved, and the burial included a proper ritual practice. People were remarkably dominant and dependent on the wild crops, hunting, and long-term food preservation with the help of a sticky soil process.

Olivia: We may not have any written documents from this time, but we found many buried skeletons with some solid carved rocks, metal tools, and wooden toys which are enough to tell its story. Some human skeletons' burial was found with dog skeletons, which shows when and how did we become closer to the dogs.

Engine: Neutral

Olivia: Neolithic period along with Natufian culture stayed alive for 8500 years and started falling in the 4th millennium B.C. People started spreading around the areas and made their way to the new worlds. By this time, sapient have learned and practiced basic crop production and agriculture, food preservation, and a tool making system.

This is the first time when people have invented 'writing'. They can save their thoughts for a longer period, even others can read and understand one person's written thoughts, now. Humans can count things for their records or inventory for the entire year.

Xing: It's amazing!

Olivia: This was just a beginning of human advancement. While Natufian culture comes to its end, few groups are now moving in the North-East and creating a great region of Mesopotamia. There was another group was evolved about the same time as the 'region of Egypt'.

BERT! Please set the time to ancient Iraq.

Base   : Station III
Time : 3100 BC
Type : Past
Speed: (Speed of Light) X 12.34
Place : Iraq

Olivia: Mesopotamia is one of the oldest known civilizations and extensions of the nearby people from the Neolithic period. With a bigger diameter including eastern Syria, Kuwait, and Iraq, they were the major downtowns of Mesopotamia.

About 5000 years ago, Mesopotamia included major cities of Uruk, Babylon, Nippur, and later, a few empire cities of Akkadian and the Assyrian culture. Sapiens who lived beneath the stars, with sky made blankets, have now started building covered shelters on this vast land. Because humans didn't have any houses before, they had now started building homes.

Understanding the continuous natural patterns, such as rain, winters, summers, they began to realize that shelters were a way of bypassing weather conditions in a positive way, whereas, they had previously thought of rain as God's punishment, and the winters as a catastrophe. While they had reacted to the seasons as weird and wondered, they later completely understood the diversities, adjusting to the seasons.

They began living in smaller groups by hunting and cultivating together. This was a great change for all of us. We could produce grains, and hunting was getting easier in groups. We had started settling down on a bigger scale for the very first time in the entire human history.

Jimmy: Yes, the same place where we just had a Time Machine trip in the future in 2003 A.D.

The site of Uruk held with countless extraordinary people who created a basic pattern for us on different matters. Some of the earliest most important developments, including the invention of the wheel, mathematics, astronomy, and agriculture, were held on this land. Today, Iraq is the mixture of Arabs and Kurds whose ancestry goes to some other mysterious group of people.

BERT: Captain! Engine is alarming red. Should I put it in neutral?

Olivia: Reboot machine and set time to Egypt.

BERT: Rebooting in 10 seconds.

Olivia: While humans from Mesopotamia were conquering the North-East, humans from Egypt were establishing a new kind of civilization in the South. People who lived here believe in rituals and an after-life eternity.

The Egyptians believed, that only special burial processes make a person to go from one side to another. 'Pharaoh', who, is also a supreme religious power in the South. Subjects obey him and in return pharaoh often provides them linen and the food.

In the early summer 3000 B.C., rain clouds began to follow, 800 miles of the Egyptian border, flood water from the mountain which made this giant river of Nile. This phenomenal, wide, and purified water makes the Nile a great legend in rivers. The Nile is 4,200 miles long and afterwards it merges with the White Nile in Sudan.

Flooding is an annual event in this region of Egypt. The first four hundred years were so special for this civilization because they have created a milestone for future humans by making engineered infrastructures and complexes. A square shaped, 50-foot-tall wall was created around the city to make its people safe by the Nile's occasional flooding in 2900 B.C. and can be seen at the West bank of the Nile today.

Menes was the first pharaoh elected by the people for their social and economic development. In the late twenty-seventh century BCE, another monumental dam by humans to divert the Nile's direction for human safety in the first time in the entire human history. This 37-foot-thick damn was created with two solid walls, made by 1200 tons of rock, and filled with sand in the middle. This could be a place where the modern 'engineering' word formed.

Xing: Apology, Professor! But it sounds awkward. In the middle of the vast desert how did they transport such a heavy quantity of rocks?

Olivia: You have a great sense of humor. The Egyptians had converted the Nile river to an interstate highway system. This pressured water flows south to north, and they made an additional East-West artificial canal system to transport passengers and goods in the city. They had started using long and shallow boats for transportation of stones, food, grains, and even humans.

The Egyptians believed that dead people need us to be with them and the tombs were their afterlife home. Initially, these tombs were created with bricks and mud.

A single tomb can have more than one burial chamber with dozens of rooms. These rectangular shaped rooms have all the amenities with what a person needs after life and is important for eternity. But, this afterlife home wasn't cheap for an ordinary civilian. If you want one of those chambers in the tomb for eternity, you must pay a huge amount.

However, very few people get an opportunity to make a proper burial chamber. The burial process included mummification of the body, a mask, a heart-shaped stone, and a symbolic writing about the person's life.

During the mummification, they take the internal organs out from the body for separate wrapping in salt and baking soda for a few days and let them dry. Once they are dried, they are wrapped, and placed along with the body in the stone coffin.

A proper mummification could take up to seventy-two days. This writing, or book of the dead, includes symbols, drawings, and colorful paintings. We have found these scrolls in every coffin excavated from this region. It took hundreds of years to decipher these symbolic words and colorful painted pictures.

Daphne: May I, Professor? But what made these documents survive even after 5000 years in the future?

Olivia: These scrolls began their lives with a papyrus plant which are plentiful along with the river Nile. They peeled the stems and pounded them into thin sheets. In a dry climate like Egypt, papyrus were extremely durable, lasting thousands of years.

Then they write and paint pictures on it. It looked so powerful and seemed like a code of human life. In the beginning of the human life, the first communication in a durably preserved, written form was the first revolutionary act for humanity.

After a long run of Egyptian civilization, in 2662 B.C. the new pharaoh name Djoser established his power on Egyptian land. He was the second pharaoh and a powerful leader in the South. He was a wise ruler and the people followed him for even after 2000 years of his death.

During his reign he was so popular that the people thought he would be immortal. He was the first human to be mummified as a God. After a few years of his oath for pharaoh, he started building a pyramid which would have his tomb and after-life home.

So far, pharaohs were making their tombs with bricks and mud. The tombs weren't successful and collapsed within a few hundred years.

Djoser was the first pharaoh who started a new kind and everlasting tomb. Djoser used big stones for the construction of his tomb, who became known as a 'God of stone' in the history books.

In Mesopotamia, much of the infrastructure was still based on bricks and mud form. This stone made infrastructure was revolutionary and the most unique thing that ever happened to humankind.

This pyramid was made at a place named Saqqara with neighbors to the capital city of Memphis. They assembled over 11,000 people to build this gigantic architectural monument. To build his after-life tomb, men worked for food, linen, and tax breaks.

Jimmy: In the 21st century A.D., modern sapiens consider Egypt as a wonder of 'the great pyramids of Giza'. There are three different pyramids which were made alongside each other.

In 2551 B.C., a new pharaoh, named 'Khufu', was elected by the people of Egypt. During his reign, he was so powerful that he had started building bigger pyramids ever in the Egyptian history. His after-life tomb (pyramid) was completed around

2540 B.C. and was 453 feet tall. Later, two more pyramids were built beside Khufu's pyramid in 1510 and 1480 B.C.

BERT: Captain! Our time is drastically elapsing.

Jimmy: Make it neutral!

Olivia: Passengers! We have seen the Neolithic period of civilization from the Mesopotamian to the Egyptian civilization. At this time both American subcontinents were unknown to the eastern world but there was one more group of people who started living together about this time. They were extremely intelligent, and their roots were about the same time as the Neolithic period of civilization.

Xing: Who were these people?

Olivia! My goodness! Please set time to Indus Valley.

Base   : Station IV
Time : 2600 BC
Type : Past
Speed: (Speed of Light) X 12.34
Place : Indus Valley

Olivia: We have been roaming around the world, travelling from modern Iraq to old Mesopotamia and the Egyptian civilization. While Mesopotamians and Egyptians were making their way towards the future race, the Indus Valley Civilization was also unknowingly competing with them simultaneously in 2600 B.C. It was one of the three oldest civilizations on our planet and nurtured between modern Afghanistan, Pakistan, and the Himalayan range to the province of Gujarat, India, today.

These sapience were peacefully living a very simple life without any fighting. They knew about counting, cultivation, and most importantly, storing things in a well-planned manner. Storage of grains and food for the entire year was the biggest success story of Harappians and for us today.

The Indus river was the main source of water and life in this Bronze Age. People were hard-working; they built Harappa and Mohenjo Daro in just under a century. These cities were remarkably architected in every manner. Archaeologists have found the same pattern of huge water storage around the city and concluded that the water collection was simply intuitive determination of supply for the entire year after flooding.

We haven't seen this kind of water savings in Mesopotamian or the Egyptian civilization yet. People understood in the beginning that water is life, which was a great step towards the modern world.

Archeologists have found many storage rooms and compared its capacity of the population, which was approximated by the number of rooms in single and double-story houses. Frequent findings of skeletons were also helpful in knowing around the 2600 B.C. census.

People were incredibly intelligent and built the entire city in a systematic manner. Covered drainage with both-sided wide pavement in between the houses, was an ultimate achievement of this group of people.

We probably don't have any written documents of this creative eastern civilization, but some writing on tablets and walls have been discovered. We have also found hundreds of carved stone statutes, marbles, and dices, as well as a big engineered water pond in the upper part of the city. This civilization was alive for 500 years and started migrating to other parts of India afterwards.

❑

Destination B
Humans on Trees

Olivia: Human children sometimes ask questions to themselves, who we are as humans, and where did we come from? That's true that we all come from our mom's tummy, but this is not a complete story.

A few hundred thousand years ago we were living our lives as an 'above-ground living creatures'. We were mutated in multiples of breeds over the course of millions of years. If we cut the crap, so there were 6-8 different breeds which helped Homo sapiens to evolve. In human extinction race, Homo sapiens outperformed all other human relatives and are the only survivors today.

Base   : Station IX

Time : 300,000 Years

Type : Past

Speed: (Speed of Light) X 12.34

Place : Congo-Africa

About 300,000 years ago humans are still jumping around and climbing over one tree to another. Hands are getting perfect to grip anything with ten solid fingers now. Feet are getting flatter and doesn't allow us to be a part of tree anymore. This natural selection gave new birth to humanity and made Chimpanzees to change their life pattern forever.

We are going to start a 'journey of life' on this vast landscape. This moment of leaving trees as shelter and buying a sky made blanket in return, doesn't seem to be a good deal. We have no option, but to leave and struggle hard to make our future race as most intelligent, social, and stronger species among all.

It was also a scary moment for all of us. By far, humans did not need any major protection to save themselves as an above ground living creature. We are in Jungles and trying to settle down on a land which is leading by wild animals.

These meat eaters fight for their territory and happy to see new immigrants from trees. These wild animals are so cruel, and humans are getting favourite buffet for their weekends. We did whatever we could do to fight with these non-vegetarian giants and deal with their sharp teeth and nails. We made pointed wooden spears, stone made small throwing weapons to save our ass.

We humans match about 40% DNA with worms, 60% with chicken, 80% with mice and nearly 100% with our closest living ancestors "the great apes". About 11 million years ago, a new kind of breed evolved, called Orangutans. These orangutans were our first distant ancestors in all ten million other living creatures on Earth and can be found in Asia today. These species match human DNA of 96.7%. Nearly 8 million years ago these creatures transformed into Gorillas slowly over 3 million years of period.

Gorillas are the largest among all the Apes, they may look like beasts, but they are very gentle and vegetarian. Gorillas can be found in sub-Saharan Africa forest today and matches human DNA of about 97.7%.

Our mutation from apes took millions of years and about five million years ago, Gorillas finally transformed to our closest ancestors on Earth as "Chimpanzees". Gorillas also split off one more breed called "Bonobo".

These chimps created a new kind of peace called "Sex". Unlimited resources in jungle and peaceful life added one more luxury to our ancient human society. Dominating wild animals were enormous in numbers but chimps are making them fall behind by sex reproduction in multiple times.

With a male dominating culture, chimps are very much alike Casanovas personality, but social. Chimps can be found in north of the Congo river today. To be honest, these distant relatives are very naughty in nature and frequent sex make them excited, to get going. Where chimps are party cousins, Bonobo spends their lives in peace in the southern part of the river.

Based on laboratory sequencing, these two species diverged around one million years ago. Both chimps and bonobo are some of the most social great apes, with social bonds occurring among individuals in large communities.

Chimps and bonobos are equally humanity's closest living relatives. As such, they are among the largest brained, and most intelligent of primates. They use a variety of sophisticated tools and construct elaborate sleeping nests each night from branches and foliage.

Both brothers have been extensively studied for their learning abilities. They are far ahead of humans in short term memory, in nutshell photo captured memory.

Xing: But what about long term memory?

Jimmy: Nada!

Chimps and bonobo matches 98.5% DNA with humans. So, what makes us humans, and them an animal? How does this 1.5% difference make them saturate in a small part of Congo, Africa, and we as humans dominate the entire planet?

Olivia: We misunderstood this change for a moment, but soon enough understood the basic pattern and properties of this new human life. As humans are walking on the ground, river, streams, and water ponds are getting closer to humankind. Nearby streams also evolve as a major source of living for daily chores.

Along with water, trees are falling just with the weight of delicious fruits. Nobody must fight because the food source is plentiful.

Hair on the human body is decreasing gradually in size, and the colour tone is becoming lighter. Humans have a smoother, attractive, and sexier body with a solid and complex, brain structure. Those 3000 hairs per square inch are still there, but, very small in size.

About 300,000 years ago, humans have finally left East-Africa to settle their future kingdoms in North Africa, Europe, and Asia. According to the nature's rule, each living creature shall evolve in multiples of breeds, in its own category. The same way, when 'Sapiens' got off the trees, they had many other brothers and sisters along with them.

After four billion years of life's life, a natural selection is sculpting human breeds in a hard way. If you can't fight, you cannot survive.

A mediocre 'archaic human' breed in-between apes and humans are often recognized as Homo Neanderthalensis (Neanderthal). Neanderthals have mainly evolved in Europe and western Asia. Their body is bulkier and more muscular than homo sapiens. The extinction of this breed evolved about 250,000 years BCE to 40,000 years BCE.

Neanderthal's strong muscular shape, with a minor, warmth blood temperature, allows them to adapt well in the cold climate of the ice age in western Eurasia.

While Europe and western Asia were populated by Hercules Neanderthalensis, the southern part of Asia evolved with a new kind of breed known as 'Homo Erectus'. Scientists are confident that Erectus is the closest genetic change in Homo sapiens.

Archaic human has also categorized humanity according to the size of the brain in our heads. To identify our brothers and sisters, homo sapiens have decided to keep measure 'the brain size' in between 1200 to 1400 cubic centimetres. The archaic human category also elaborates its base on the age of the hominid society. Archaic human also categorized other cousins as Homo Solensis, 'man from solo valley', Homo Floresiensis, and Homo Denisova.

The eastern part is now hostile for these breeds, but at this time, East Africa also had nurtured multiples of human breeds such as Homo Rudolfensis, 'Man from Lake Rodolf', Homo Ergaster, 'Working man' and of course, homo sapiens the 'Wise man'.

It doesn't really matter, as under God's command, every human being needs to survive in negative consequences, such as global, or manmade calamities.

About a hundred thousand years ago, the census on a pie chart, showed that some human breeds were enormous in numbers, and some were in low populations.

A few human breeds started hunting in a preplanned way with the help of friends, and some started gathering only special varieties of wild grains. Out of all the human species, some of them only lived on a single island, while some of them made their way to different parts of the world.

Because all these cousins belong to the same genus, 'Homo', the genetic life chain describes that Homo Erectus were the descendants of Homo Ergaster, which transformed into Homo Neanderthalensis, and eventually Neanderthal, which evolved into Homo Sapiens.

Now it's time for battle; battle for existence, to rule the world, and humanity. There were many cousins around who shared the same genus as 'Homo', and everybody had an opportunity to prove their special creation's worth to their god.

Perhaps, the Gods didn't like this idea of the biggest blood shed for their own survival. Different human breeds were fighting for their territory, food reserves, and in the worst case, humiliation also takes place. Other than humans, wild animals still aren't not too behind to lose any chance to make human life into their meal.

The reason and cause behind the survival of humanity is a shield which protects us, to grow under it, often called, 'mother nature'. Anything and everything follows its command to all its lives. All those oxygen, carbon, and natural minerals we take in our lives, would have to return it back to nature to balance the ledger.

A weird thing happened to all kinds of life, including humans about 74,000 years ago. Toba super volcano erupted millions and billions of tons of poisonous gas, smoke, and hot lava, almost wiping out all kinds of life on Earth, including humans.

Immense carbon dioxide in the atmosphere built a huge greenhouse gas effect, effectually trapping sunlight that led to never-ending winters. It was about 500 years to 1000 years of without Sun and extreme winter made most of the cousins end their heritage forever. Most of the vegetation and fat animals died first.

Genetic evidences are suggesting that all humans are the descendants from the very few survivors of this volcanic eruption, of about 800 to 1000 humans that majorly included Homo Sapiens, Homo Erectus, & Homo Neanderthalensis.

After a long race of survival, Erectus' and Neanderthals started lacking behind in long term memories, hunting tactics, and skills in surviving in harsh weather.

In 30,000 BCE, humans are unknown, but global warming is still affecting the Earth in different ways, as in climate, geological, and biological changes. Out of dozens of 'Genus-homo' breeds, 'Sapience' were the only survivor in the continuously changing climates, which is drastically warming up the environment, necessitating special qualities and techniques to survive in different parts of the world. At this time, only the homo sapiens breed was able to survive, leaving everyone (homo-genus breeds) to fall behind in the entire human extinction of survival.

Time: 25,000 Years

Place: Garden of Eden

Type: Past

BERT: Passenger! Please, look through the right window.

Olivia: A hairless human female is taking a shower under this falling stream. It's a bright, shiny morning, and she's beautiful. Her parents were too hairy, but it is just a natural transformation under our ozone shield. These reduced hairs had taken place, just because of our natural environmental change due to global warming.

Eve's senses are on alert. She's attentive and has a couple of weapons nearby on a rock in case of an unprovoked attack.

She's never seen any other human either; male or female, other than herself. She has a feeling that perhaps God made someone for her.

About 20 years ago from this very moment, there was another homo erupts couple who gave birth to a hairless male human child. He was later in the Hebrew scriptures called Adam. One day Adam was passing by the Garden of Eden and saw the beauty of the flowers and trees filled with luscious fruits. It was a big day for him, as he had already planned to bring all his hairy family to this place and live in peace with plenty of food. This was the time when homo erupts breed were making hairless humans. Different changes also include changes in the human brain, eye structure, and the DNA itself, which was changing constantly.

Our skull from homo erupts was just a little extra on the back of our heads. Our facial jaw was a little bit big, too. But after a constant change of our skull and jaw structure from ancestors of trees to homo eructs until homo sapiens was great. Our head part was changed completely, which helped in enhancing the long-term memory. The human's head transformed upwards and has extra internal space to carry a bigger and bigger brain organ. The jaw bones are getting smaller for proper working and use of our vocal cords.

This was a great and special moment for humanity, especially for the homo sapiens breed. The relationship between Adam and Eve emerged to a next level of love, which eventually gave birth to entire hairless boys.

Some of the greatest scientists think that 'gods' have cloned the homo sapiens from the DNA of our nearest ancestors. They came here with a plan, therefore, it's a huge possibility that Adam and Eve were 'avatars' brought by Gods directly from heaven if they didn't go through the artificial genetic processes from our cousins. The sacred holy scriptures descriptions were recorded long ago for us to understand today.

❑

Destination C
Reign of Religion

Olivia: The starting point for religion was to keep the culture and society under one flag representing a group of people, places, or beliefs. A belief system under a religion usually came, either from a person, or a God.

Protecting religion from outsiders who can damage its society insignificantly for gold, personal belongings or maybe for a woman. It was very important for humans to understand the group belief system to contribute their share and protect women, children, and older people of the society.

The diversification of different religions was made so that they could identify themselves in different groups. This process of isolation from other kinds of groups was later called as 'religion'.

Religion was lovely, and people now have a door through which they can at least imagine, pray, and complete a 'one-way communication' to a God.

Xing: But Professor! What happened, how did all these civilizations disappear in India and other places?

Jimmy: These humans didn't disappear but merged with another kind of humans who were trying to give a more systematic and arranged life in a democratic way on this vast land. Instead of a couple of cities, the Aryans were dreaming for something bigger in a civilization which could break the boundaries wanting to make a huge country.

Olivia: By far, the Egyptians and Mesopotamians have an economy which is run by a few religious leaders, kings, or queens. But, on this eastern subcontinent, the Aryans had created a new line of democracy for equality. They believed that humans live this life for a divine purpose. The equality they had believed was scattered in different groups of people. They called it as a multiple cast system.

Again, we must remember the census of this time was about a thousand times lower than present. Today, our lives are surrounded by machineries, and they do mass production for us.

The Aryans accepted this as an opportunity to collaborate people for the same purpose as a happy life. They had created an economy which has different groups of people with expertise in only one or two areas to produce more in a collective way.

For an example, if you make good chairs, you can do it and you are going to be in 'Badai' group. If you make iron swords or antiques, you are going to be called a 'Lohar'; if you are cleaning the garbage or dirt, they'll call you a 'Chamaar'. Nobody forced them, but they chose to do these jobs in accordance to the wage against it.

Later, population (over population) drastically grew. While the population grew, they jumbled in jobs and skills, taking them away from their ancestry origin group. They had accepted this life style and started their contribution to the economy towards more production.

This newly found group as Aryans has now started connecting different societies under one flag, covering almost the entire Pakistan and modern India. As an individual civilian, localists are getting a chance to be a part of the contributing society. The Aryans are dreaming to fill India in different colours of life, and as an easy simple communicative language with perfect grammar known as 'Sanskrit'.

The Aryans also brought in education, language, farming skills, astronomy, culture, rituals, festivals, cultivation, stories, and much more.

Hinduism (Sanatan) however, builds its world on the results of spiritual and astronomical practices. Like their name, they were the most intelligent and creative humans so far on Earth. Unlike the Mesopotamians and Egyptians, the Aryans had a completely different notion towards life.

Some leftover troops from the Indus Valley civilization were still trying to settle down on the same land, but with a modern life style. They were highly impressed with a new kind of a simplified communication language brought in by the Aryans.

About 1520 BC, they started writing their first holy scripture called 'Vedas'. Vedas had four separate volumes. 'Rig veda' was one of the first volumes completed in 1475 BCE. Other scriptures such as Vedas, Upnishads, Puraanas, Upanyaas, Vedanga, and most importantly, Surya Sidhanta, were written afterwards.

According to scriptures, the whole universe is created by Brahama, Vishnu, and Mahesh. They had then created the first human as 'Manu' to serve his divine purpose.

People often refer Mahesh as Lord Shiva and know him to be as a 'destroyer'. Brahma as a 'creator' and Vishnu as 'preserver' are primal philosophies of Hindu scholars. The scriptures clearly mentioned that they had extreme powers and came from the sky on their shiny crafts (Vimana).

These supersonic Gods also have the power to create Avatars to help humanity. Later, Lord Rama and Krishna were born as Avatars for a divine purpose. They took birth in front of the people and fought for some reason to fulfill the Gods' will.

"In Hindu society, it is a religious custom, first thing in the morning, to bathe in a nearby river or at home if no river or stream is at hand. People believe that it makes them holy. Then still without having eaten, they go to the temple and make offerings of flowers and cubical and spherical sugar sweets to the local God. Some will wash the idol and decorate it with red and yellow powder. Nearly every home has a corner or even a room for worship of the family's favourite God. A popular God in some localities is Ganesha, the elephant god. People will especially pray to him for good fortune, as he is known as a remover of obstacles. In other places Krishna, Rama, Shiva, Durga or some other deity might take first place in devotion." - Tara C., Kathmandu, Nepal.

Today, India's door is open for every religion and culture. Friendly behaviour and an intelligent mind makes Indian humans remarkable.

Today we also know India for Taj Mahal, which was built in 1643 A.D. by Mughal emperor Shah Jahan. Taj Mahal is also known as a symbol of love and was built in the name of his beloved wife Mumtaz Mahal right after her death. This architectural monument was built entirely with fine marbles, costing about 900 million USD at that time.

There are multiple Hindu texts which defines the different aspects of science today. All around the globe, many scientists are deciphering all these codes today which were thrown back as mythology by Hindus themselves.

Jimmy: Like Aryans were trying to transform a scattered place into one nation, a few other groups evolved as religion. The thoughts towards the religion was unique and created naturally.

Different religions were emerged with different groups, all around the globe, for a different purpose. Religion is a modern world for humans. In the beginning it was a new way to gather people under one type of belief system, human life, and its creation.

In the past, few wise people came in to our lives and helped us to find a God kind relief. There are considerable amounts of questionable figures associated with all these heroes who don't even believe their existence. Non-religious humans have less faith in revelations, messages, dreams, and day visions given by Gods in ancient times.

Olivia: Today, a sapient begins its life around the age of five or six, when he starts the understanding of reality. While learning about reality, we are undertaken by some imaginary fantasy world.

At the age of six, our notion towards this world are completely alien to our parents and others. But we still try harder and ask questions to our elders. Sometimes we get the answer but most of the times, no, or wrong answers, provided by our elders.

Finally, we end up with today's sophisticated video games. In twenty-one century A.D., children are surrounded by many advanced technological based games. Humans have found this age as an opportunity to mislead these innocent children to a different, almost unreal, graphics-based games.

Sapient species worked very hard and developed from a fairy tale videography to MP4 to HD, 3D, and finally 4K supported games and devices. Today we know many imaginary and fantasized heroes like He-man, Batman, or Superman.

We follow them while we are growing up and hope to help ourselves with this cruel world. Inspiration through a family member for a God to follow becomes dull and faithless at this time.

Few extraordinary heroes came to our lives and fought for us. They just didn't fight for us but died in their immortality for our freedom. It is true, these heroes died long ago, but they have left their words and writing behind. They might not have a modern muscle shaped structure, but they had a potential to make people happy by giving them a god kind of relief and satisfaction. These leaders were outstanding and unique to the ancient human society. In the beginning of sapient life, they set a pattern for the future generation in kindness, truthfulness, and confidence in one creator.

Base   : Station V

Time : 3609 Years

Type : Past

Speed: (Speed of Light)X 12.34

Place : Egypt

Human: Moses

Olivia: In the early seventeen century BC, there was a great flood in the Jordan River, forcing Israelites to migrate in the neighbourhood region of Egypt. After 1500 hundred years, afterlife believers in Egypt, become a great power in the South.

They are rich in customs and wealth. The Nile wasn't just providing them with plentiful water for irrigation and cultivation, but also providing them with an easy transportation system. The popularity of the Egyptians is becoming widespread as the greatest power and kingdom in the South.

Ramsey - 'the great', is the last pharaoh of the Egyptian kingdom, making hundreds of stone-carved monumental giants. An unlimited amount of construction work demanded hundreds of thousands of slaves and workers. Due to the flood, the migrated Jews have no choice but to work for the construction projects as a slave, and in return, earn bread for their children and families.

Eventually, Egyptians were started falling behind in numbers by international workers in construction projects. This was the time when infant children were being put into death for immorality.

Scared slave couples had no choice but to leave their infant son, Moses, in a wooden basket, and let the great river of Nile subjectively decide his future. The helpless father and mother are crying while they are saying their final good-bye and getting apart from their baby. They didn't know this child will become a prince of Egypt one day or that three great religions will follow his extraordinary teachings.

Moses was born in 1593 B.C. at a Jewish couple's compartment in the region of Egypt. Pharaoh's daughter's personal council members found this basket in no time, handing it over to the princes. The Queen adopted him as her own child and made him one of the stakeholders to claim the 'Egyptian throne' in the future.

A few years have passed, and superstitious ritual made the king to look for future power in the Egyptian kingdom. In order to complete this ritual, the king has presented two plates, one with a crown and another with hot lava, in front of young Moses in order to choose one.

Choosing the crown instead of lava would take this little child's life away. This was a great moment for humanity and undoubtably, Moses chose the lava, instead. He has burnt his fingers and immediately took his fingers into his mouth and also burnt his tongue completely. After burning his tongue Moses wasn't able to talk all his life properly.

After this ritual, the King became relaxed and looked towards the ongoing construction.

Eventually, Moses's life got easy and he started taking part in Egyptian rituals, taught by his new mother, and other masters. Prince Moses has all the amenities and luxury of modern Egyptian life. Even as a prince, Moses often goes for a walk outside of the palace, feeling the pain of other Jewish slaves.

Modern scholars claim, he had left the palace when he was twenty years old, fleeing to the Sinai Mountains, hundreds of miles from the Egyptian region. Moses lived in the mountains for six decades.

In all these 60 years, Moses developed courage to get the Jewish community freedom, and helped them migrate from the Egyptian land, and settle them back to Canaan (Deuteronomy 6:23, 34:10).

After this kind act, Moses became a prophet, judge, leader, and historian in the Israelite community. The law that Israel accepted consisted of Ten words, or commandments, over 600 laws that amounted to a comprehensive catalog of directions and guidance for daily conduct. It involved the mundane and the holy - the physical and the moral requirements, as well as the worship of God. Thus, the Jewish religion began to take definite shape, and the Jews became a nation organized for the worship and service of their God.

Ten Commandments
(Translation from original Hebrew scriptures)

- *You shall have no other gods.*

- *You shall not make for yourself a sculptured image, or any likeness of what is in the heavens above, or on the Earth below, or in the waters under the Earth. You shall not bow down to them or serve them.*

- *You shall not swear falsely by the name of your lord.*

- *Remember the sabbath day and keep it holy. The lord blessed the sabbath day and hollowed it.*

- *Honor your father and your mother.*

- *You shall not murder.*

- *You shall not commit adultery.*

- *You shall not steal.*

- *You shall not bear false witness against your neighbor.*

- *You shall not covet your neighbor's house, wife, male, or female slave. Ox or his ass, or anything that is your neighbor's.*

Moses didn't agree with different Egyptian pharaoh godship's and after life eternity. He believed, that, there is only one almighty and supreme power, who holds the Earth and universe stable.

After settling down in Canaan, Moses started writing books in order to make people understand about super power. The first five books of the Bible are accountable and written by Moses during his reign. These five books were later called as "Pentateuch" and written in the last forty years of his life.

He started writing his first book of "Genesis" in 1510 B.C. creating four additional books: Exodus, Leviticus, Numbers, and Deuteronomy until his last days. He couldn't finish his book of Deuteronomy, but the Jews later finished with the true story of his last days. Moses was one of mankind's leader who died at the age of 120 in 1473 B.C.

BERT: Captain! Time for evaporation.

Olivia: put it on Neutral.

Type: Neutral

Olivia: 2 BCE, Israel has become a central marketplace of majority of the Jewish people. Another 15 centuries have gone, and Moses's death and his commandments are still alive among the followers.

People believe that God had spoken to him, and under his commandment, Moses was able to help the Jewish people to migrate back to the Canaan. People also believed the Bible's Pentateuch books and 10 commandments are directly God's words.

A new era has begun in 1510 BCE. Word 'Religion', is spreading all around like a plague. People have at least something to follow. They can also have a satisfactory one-sided conversation with god now.

During the great biblical writing, a spectacular thing happened when Moses wrote some prophesies in his books to be happened in the future. After his death in 1473 B.C., the Jewish people were now sheltered by a nation with law (10 commandments), prosperity, and a long wait for a time, when these prophecies written by Moses become true.

The Bible is a collection of 66 different books which was written by 40 different writers over the course of 1600 years from 1510 B.C. to 98 A.D. These 40 writers, including Moses, aren't actually professional writers, but they had different professions separate than their great biblical writing.

They wrote everything, whatever they thought to be written for the future race. Other extraordinary writers were mainly fishermen, doctors, farmers, shepherds, and some were in the profession of law, and carpentry. The entire Bible was originally written in the ancient Hebrew and Greek languages and later on, it was translated into the English language for a better understanding of our modern Christian believers.

Bible scholars see these Holy Scriptures of the Bible in two parts; the New Testament and the Old Testament. The New testament was written right after Jesus' birth from 2 B.C. to 98 A.D. and includes not even one-fourth of the actual Bible. The Old Testament has compiled a history before Jesus' birth, and beyond.

Due to nature's law and biometrics body structure, we are bounded by our life-time limit of "The Hundred years", as these writers were also given the same age-coupon as we have today. These musician writers played an ultimate harmony composition by writing these important history books for mankind.

As a twenty-first century sapient, we probably don't believe in "Prophesy" but it did happen to humans several times in the past.

Base : Station VI

Time : 2 BC

Type : Past

Speed: (Speed of Light) X 12.34

Place : Jerusalem, Israel

Human: Jesus

Out of 40 great writers, Isaiah was born in the 8th century and started prophesizing in 740 B.C. In the kingdom of Judah, the Prophet Isaiah is known as a great prophet, and was presently writing a message for future generations.

He doesn't know yet, but he is going to write his book for the next forty-four years. In his book, chapter number 13 and verses 19 and 20 were written in 732 B.C. and he is writing it now.

Hebrew	English
כב; וְקַמְתִּי עֲלֵיהֶם, נְאֻם יְהוָה צְבָאוֹת. וְהִכְרַתִּי לְבָבֶל שֵׁם וּשְׁאָר, וְנִין וָנֶכֶד—נְאֻם-יְהוָה	And I will rise up against them, saith the LORD of hosts, and cut off from Babylon name and remnant, and offshoot and offspring, saith the LORD.

כג; וְשַׂמְתִּיהָ לְמוֹרַשׁ קִפֹּד, וְאַגְמֵי-מָיִם
וְטֵאטֵאתִיהָ
בְּמַטְאֲטֵא הַשְׁמֵד, נְאֻם יְהוָה צְבָאוֹת. {ס}

I will also make it a possession for the bittern, and pools of water; and I will sweep it with the besom of destruction, saith the LORD of hosts.

יט, וְהָיְתָה בָבֶל צְבִי מַמְלָכוֹת, תִּפְאֶרֶת גְּאוֹן כַּשְׂדִּים,
כְּמַהְפֵּכַת אֱלֹהִים, אֶת-סְדֹם וְאֶת-עֲמֹרָה.

"And Babylon, the most decoration (glorious) of kingdoms,
The beauty and the pride of the Chaldeans,
Will be like Sodom and Gomorrah when God overthrew them.
She will never be inhabited, nor will she be a place to reside in throughout all generations.
No Arab will pitch a tent there, and no shepherds will rest their flocks there."

Prophecy by Isaiah wasn't just accurate as it happened, but the way it will destroy. He also wrote, who will be conquering for establishment.

Many Bible prophecies have already come true. For example, Isaiah prophesied that Babylon would be destroyed. (Isaiah 13:19) He described exactly how the city would be defeated.

The city was protected by large gates and a river. But Isaiah foretold that the river would be dried up and the gates left open. The attackers would take the city without a battle. Isaiah even prophesied that a man named Cyrus would defeat Babylon. (Isaiah 44:27 - 45:2)

The Holy Scriptures weren't written to teach science or ignore science. But when it comes to scientific matters, it is always accurate. For example, the book of Leviticus contains God's instructions on ways the Israelites could stop disease from spreading. This was written long before people knew how bacteria and viruses cause disease. The Bible also correctly teaches that the Earth hangs on nothing. (Job 26:7)

The New Testament often speaks about Jesus' teachings, life, and God. Jesus' birth was mystical, as the virgin Mary gave him birth out of nowhere. Then the conspiracy of his murder added a new layer of fear around his life.

Xing: Was he the promised Messiah of Hebrew prophecy?

Olivia: The New Testament was majorly written by his disciples. One of his close disciple and biographer, Matthew, was a former Jewish tax collector. The verses written by him spell out Abraham's line of descendants down to Jacob, who became the father to Joseph, the husband of Mary, of whom Jesus was born, who is called 'Christ'.

Jesus has fulfilled many prophesies written about him (messiah) in the Old Testament. When Jesus was about thirty years old, he started his public ministry. Firstly, he went to his cousin, 'John', who often baptized Jews in the Jordan River in symbol of repentance.

Now when all the people were baptized, Jesus also was baptized and, as he was praying, the heaven was opened up and the Holy Spirit in bodily shape like a dove came down upon him, and a voice came out of heaven saying, "You are my beloved son in whom I am well pleased." - Luke 3:21-23; John 1:32-34

It was a wonderful day when Jesus went to Mount Hermon with his disciples Peter, James, and John, who were fisherman from Galilee. "And he was transfigured before them, and his face shone as the Sun, and his outer garments became brilliant as light. Look! a bright cloud overshadowed them, and, look! a voice out of the cloud, saying: 'this is my son, the beloved, whom I have approved; listen to him.' The disciples were very much afraid by hearing this." - Matthew 17:1-6, Luke 9:28-36

Jimmy: Later, Jesus was arrested and put on trial by the Jewish religious society, who falsely accused him of calling himself the 'Son of God'. (Matthew 26:3,4; 59-67)

The Jews didn't have enough authority to punish Jesus, so they sent him to the Roman rulers. Now, Jesus has been passed from one ruler to another, the Roman governor, Pontius Pilate, on the insistence of the religiously inspired mob, who took the line of least resistance and sentenced Jesus to death.

This was a tragic moment for Christian followers who felt abandoned and despair at the sentencing, but at the same time, they are still motivated with Jesus' sayings. Christianity had captured the world where the teaching for forgiveness lent a new way of seeing such matters through a different lens to the compassion of Christ's heart, such as the woman caught in adultery.

Writing in the sand, her accusers left one by one until all were gone at Jesus' stark words, "He who is without sin, cast the first stone." My question is: The man was equally caught in adultery, but it was the woman who was seen as being sinful. A man's world, indeed, that Jesus wasn't afraid to confront head-on! In the twenty-first century, Christians are about one in three in the world's entire population.

Type: Neutral - (Monotheism-polyphasic)

Olivia: Another six hundred years have gone. Christians and Jews are still fighting over their gods and beliefs. There were many prophesies about Jesus as 'Messiah' in the old scriptures, and Jesus himself never denied Moses' teachings. So, then why don't people mind their own religion?

In the beginning, we had seen Egyptians in how they believed in after life eternity in 3100 BC. Things became changed when

Moses disagreed with after-life rituals and practices. According to him, God cherished us so that we can live and enjoy our surroundings, not to die for eternity. We can be immortal, only if we live our lives. It was a great moment when Moses started this great Biblical writing in 1510 BCE. His teachings were simply based in one creator, 'Monotheism'.

After 1500 years of Moses' death, people have changed their notion completely when Jesus told them 'He is the only son of God, who they have been praying all their lives'. In reference to the Bible, Jesus performed hundreds of miracles in front of hundreds of people. In real, these many people can't be wrong. Everybody agreed with his teachings and recorded as the 'New Testament in the Bible'.

Base : Station VII

Time : 570 AD

Type : Past

Speed: (Speed of Light)X 12.34

Place : Mecca

Human: Muhammad

Olivia: But after millions of followers, there was one young man in Arab, who didn't agree that Jesus was the 'son of God'. In the beginning of the seventh century, Islam spread all over northern Africa to the West, and eastwards unto Pakistan, India, and Bangladesh. Islam also made its effect down to Indonesia at this time.

Muhammad's teachings involved the faith in 'one creator' as 2000 years ago Sir Moses described. 'Monotheism' is the primary building blocks of Islam. God is only one and only one. He doesn't need any son to communicate with human beings.

'In the name of Allah; the beneficent, the merciful'. In Quran it continues with; 'Praise to be Allah, Lord of the worlds; The beneficent, the merciful; owner of the day of Judgement. Thee (alone) we worship; Thee (alone) we ask for help. Show us the straight path; The path of those whom thou hast favoured; Not (the path) of those who earn Thine anger nor of those who go astray.' The Quran, Surah 1:1-7

About 1400 years ago, a man was born right here in Mecca, in Saudi Arabia who had changed the picture of God completely as it was changed back in Jesus' and as well as in Moses' time.

Muhammad was the last of a long line of prophets, who brought God amongst humanity. He just wasn't a spiritual genius, but a great leader. He created a religion, Islam, which was followed by his followers' right after his death.

Olivia: There are a few written sources which are crucial for Islamic life and in which Muhammad often plays a heroic character. The first is the Quran itself, Islam's holy book. There is also a rich library of stories and sayings about Muhammad's life.

The holy revelations given by the God 'Allah' through the angel name 'Gabriel' directly to Muhammad, is preserved and written down, right after his death. The other prestigious sources are available as 'Hadith'. Muhammad was a very important man and by the time he died, he had hundreds of thousands of Islamic followers.

So, right now we are in this library and these books are filled with Muhammad's life and his journey for mankind. There is a section where we keep some non-Muslims sources and books about Muhammad. Some of the non-Muslim accounts proves his presence as a powerful leader in the year of 630 AD.

Muhammad was born on April 22nd, 571AD at mecca city which has been ruled by a tribe over the centuries, 'the Quraysh'. His father died before his birth and his mother was very poor.

Before Muhammad's birth all the tribes, in Arabia found a place, which they thought, built by the god, the pilgrimage. People at that time belicved, the pilgrimage was initially made by Adam under the God's command.

Kabah (Pilgrimage) later kept and placed over 360 different Gods (idols) in it by Muhammad. This was his small contribution to mankind that, 'God is actually one'. Idol prayer or multiple God system is not right, we all shall believe in almighty, who is one and over rule this world.

Each follower has his own right to connect with his God by circling the Kabah. There was a special type of truth declared that all hostile tribes can come together to mecca to circle the Kabah and worship their Gods without fear and conflict.

Arabic's preserved all this information and messages given by Muhammad, preserved in their daily lives and prayers. The Quran was written about a decade after Muhammad's death. People have been following him and remember all of his sayings.

While the Hadith was still debating over this, there are remarkably hundreds of examples available with non-Muslim sources. Non-Muslim evidence for Muhammad is not copied; it exists. Muhammad name exits in Greek, Syriak, and opinion writings.

A Greek historian wrote about him after 24 years of his death. The particular interest here is that first time someone talked about Muhammad, about his name, and what he did. This book is talking about the year of 630 A.D. which was even before Muhammad's death.

"A certain man whose name was Muhammad, a merchant as if by the command of God, appeared to them as a preacher. Now, Muhammad gave them rose, namely, not to eat curium, not to drink wine, not to speak false words, and not to engage in fornication."

Non-Muslim accounts wrote the same thing around the same time as Muslim accounts. We know he was born in a city, ruled by a tribe in Mecca, and that the Quraysh and his family was poor. His father died before he was born, left his mother, Amina, when he was a few months old, when she handed him over to a tribe on an outskirt of Mecca, which was a tradition of that time. Muhammad's first four years of his life was miserable.

Arabia, at the time of Muhammad's birth, was cruel to live. There was no law, no state, and very little peace. Tribal loyalty and custom relationship was the only source of protection. Justice was harsh, arbitrary, and the punishment was brutal. A man for example, can be killed for a loaf of bread. Daily struggle for survival left very little room in compassion for most people, and very little chance for a better existence.

This age of ignorance give birth to a legend as Muhammad. He has assembled all the hundreds of smaller tribes in Arabia and merge into one as Aryans did it in 2000 BCE in India. The society was structured to a belief system, but also, we should understand that organized religion today.

This is 570 CE and people in Arabia are believing in many God systems. Every tribe had their own favorite God and Mecca, Muhammad's birth place, is believed to be the most important central place of this polytheistic world.

Orthodox Muslims believed that Kabah was built by God at the time of Adam, but there's no archeological or historical evidence to confirm its exact origins. Muslim sources acknowledge that the Kabah was the central place of worship of God existing from the time of Adam. Then it was rebuilt by Abraham and his son Ismael whose ancestry was same as Jesus Christ.

There is no non-Muslim source which can connect Abraham to Mecca. This regular pilgrimage brought many people to Mecca and that meant there was opportunity for trade and wealth.

Muhammad was born, one of the biggest tribes at this time, 'Quraysh'. They control running of the Kabah so that rich & powerful, although Muhammad's immediate family were not the part of the ruling elite.

At the age of 5, Muhammad returned to his mother, Amina, in Mecca but her health wasn't well. She decided to visit her family in Yathrib, 300 kms north of Mecca, but the camel ride made her illness worse. She didn't survive, and Muhammad was alone in the world now.

The young Muhammad was to learn even more about loss and sorrow. Right after Amina's death, Muhammad was sheltered by his only uncle 'Abu Thalib', who was a powerful person in Meccan elite.

Abu Thalib is a successful trader, taking caravans to Syria, part of the business in ancient time connected Arabia to the popular centres of the civilization of middle east and beyond. Mecca is just a link in this chain and emerged as central hub.

For Muslims, 'Mecca' is a central market place at this time. Muslim tradition gives us an important support for Mecca and its great trading. Muhammad was involved in this early caravan trading, where he was subjected to contact with the outside world. The place of travel was through the desert and oasis in Arabian towns.

By the time Muhammad became 21, he had gain the reputation and integrity known as 'Alamin', the honest and truthful one.

So, what did Muhammad, entering his prime face, look like? Muslim tradition prohibits any portrait/picture of him. We do have some detailed written accounts, describing his biography.

'A little above average height, he had a 30 build with long muscular limps and tapering fingers. His hair was long, thick and wavy, his eyes were large and black with a touch of brown, his beard was thick, he was a fair complexion, and now ready to get married.'

Muhammad was married to an old, rich woman named, 'Khadijah', and also did some business for her in Syria. Muhammad, as a prophet himself, did a great step of his life as we do today in western world. It's rare to marry with a younger man, but in Muhammad's day, it was almost unheard of.

In most of Arabia women, before coming to Islam were treated as animals and with few human rights. But the city life, merchant life gives women opportunities.

Muhammad's marriage with Khadijah lasted for 24 years. Khadijah's presence shows women has an equal hand in Islamic evolution.

He often goes to a nearby, mountain cave (Ghar Hira) for meditation. According to the Muslim tradition, one day when he was there, an angel, later identified as Gabriel, commanded him to recite in the name of Allah. Muhammad failed to respond, so the angel caught him forcefully and pressed him so hard that he could not bear it anymore; then the angel repeated the command. Again, Muhammad failed to react, so the angel chocked him again. This occurred three times before Muhammad started to recite what came to be viewed as the first of a series of revelations that constitute the holy Quran.

Eventually, Muhammad achieved dominance when Mecca surrendered to him in January of 630 A.D. and he became its ruler.

Since people weren't friendly with professional paper making, they used shoulder blades of camel, palm leaves, wood, and parchment to write, procure, and preserve God's words as Quran. After his death, the Arabs collected all the shoulder blades, leaves, and wood; people who have still memorized Muhammad's sayings.

Islam spread all over the world and established a belief which was crucial towards a 'one creator' philosophy. Today, Muslims are about two billion in number with the ratio of 1 in 6 of the world population.

"Almost all the historical narratives of Quran have their biblical parallels... Among the Old Testament characters, Adam, Noah, and Abraham are mentioned about seventy times in twenty-five different surahs. Moses' name appeared in thirty-four different surahs. The story of creation and the fall of Adam is mentioned five times, the flood, eight, and Sodom eight. New Testament characters, Zachariah, John the Baptist, Jesus (Isa), and Mary are also very much included in holy Quran."

Muhammad's successor after his death was a big question. A prophet's death brought a new crisis to humanity. He died without any son or any clear successor.

The successor of the prophet would be a caliph, khalifah, or ruler. The legitimate successor was nominated in between Abu Bakr (Muhammad's father in law), Umer (the prophet's advisor), and the Uthman (the prophet's son in-law).

Muslims believe that a dead person's soul goes to the barzakh, or 'partition', 'the place or state in which people will be after death and before judgement'. (Surah 23:99,100) The soul is conscious there experiencing what is termed the 'Chastisement of the Tomb' if the person has been wicked or enjoying happiness if he had been faithful ones must also experience some torment because of their few sins while alive. On the judgement day, each faces his eternal destiny, which ends that intermediate state.

In contrast, the righteous are promised heavenly gardens of paradise: 'And as for those who believe and do good works, we shall make them enter gardens underneath, which rivers flow to dwell therein forever.' (Surah 4:57)

It was actually the right and obvious thing for mankind. 4000-year-old religion has overruled the 300,000-year-old humanity in order to save humanity. These ancient civilizations and religions became an important part of our human society.

❑

Destination D
The only 'Shield'

Time: 300 Million Years
Type: Past

Olivia: This seems to be like another imaginary planet. But in reality, we have a deep connection with this alien-like place. This is a beautiful, shiny day. Feeling this shiny light from the Sun on our faces gives us 'energy' as a form of Vitamin D which will last for the rest of the day, or perhaps the next few days, or maybe forever, nobody knows.

Energy never dies but can be transferred from one source to another. Our only source of energy is the Sun, which has been continuously striking its energy to Earth from last 4.5 billion years. Imagine this beautiful, shiny day that we're feeling with this light on our face which has been created about hundreds of thousand years ago.

Xing: Captain! But how this energy is related to humans? How could this relate to our human age and where did we come from?

Olivia: Without this energy, our planet is an empty room. Anything and everything needs this supernatural fuel to run. The water in oceans, fruits on trees, trees in forests, and blood in bones, begged all their lives for this particle. If this energy would abandon us one day, there is no way that oceans can flow, forests, or even humans, can survive on this planet.

BERT: There would be no life, no birds, and no flowers. It's an ultimate monopoly, which we all have to obey since our birth to our death. Even a 'machine' needs energy to run.

Olivia: The quantity of solar energy we get today in a single day on our planet is sufficient enough to nurture the entire mankind from the past and future. The Sun generates tremendous amounts of energy per second, let's say a hundred billion; atomic bombs are bursting per second inside Sun.

Because of the ozone layer, most of the light and energy reflect in other directions. The only energy and light we get on the ground is extremely filtered with a blue ozone layer around the surface.

This layer is amazing. Now life can breathe under this shield. We can assume the Earth and its protective ozone layer are perfect for humanity. For example, we need food to live and grow, and notably, the ozone also gets energy so that Earth can breathe, including us, as well as other, living creatures. From the point where the ozone starts, its boundary to the surface of the Earth is called the "atmosphere".

This is the reason when we see upwards in the day time, our blue atmosphere glows with sunlight, appearing as a blue sky. After 4.5 billion years, now, intelligent life, like humans, evolved because of the ozone followed by the atmosphere's perfect conditions. We are opening our eyes when the global warming is on its peak.

This ozone is a knight for the heavenly kingdom of human beings on Earth. It can let only good vibes and rays come across its boundary to the Earth's surface. The Sun's delivery to our door as sunlight, including photons, energy, carbon, and other particles, slow down thousands of times when they cross this ozone layer.

Xing: Captain! But what if this oxygen layer wasn't existed?

Olivia: There is absolutely no chance to survive under those circumstances. Our Earth's atmosphere is bounded by the ozone layer around it. In the absence of the atmosphere, wind wouldn't blow in the air, the ocean circulatory system will be shut down, and atoms and particles will vanish by the Sun's deadly, ultraviolet rays in no time. This ozone is actually the only real shield of life on our planet.

Daphne: Captain! Is there any expiry date on this shield or would it be lasting forever?

Olivia: The challenge is that, the 'ozone' can be damaged anytime by internal or external hazards. Internal hazards include our own 'atmosphere' which breathes under the ozone umbrella. The atmosphere usually depends on the different geographical patterns, or areas such as tropical, mountains, ocean, desert, or rain forest.

BERT: Our Sun has grown 10% since its birth and is still getting bigger day by day. As a result of its increasing size, the Earth is also getting warmer on a daily basis. The Earth was never being warmer like this before, ever, or since.

External hazards, including deadly solar flares, CME (Corona Mass Ejection) wave, cosmic wave, asteroids, and the continuous bombardment of meteorites, can damage our Earth at any time.

In the twenty-first century, humans are also affected by carbon emissions. People still have no choice but to run motor vehicles, factories, machineries, and technologies to fulfill their needs and wants. So actually, humans are destroying our atmosphere on a daily basis by adding increasingly carbon atoms to it.

The ozone can be damaged in few minutes, but recovery could take up to hundreds of years to regain its shape. This recovery period doesn't carry any life around. So, as humans, it is very important for us to make every effort to protect our atmosphere and ozone as well.

It would cost us the 'end of life' on Earth if we fail to obey this rule. We are probably feeling safe today, but the amount we are damaging this layer, our future generations would have less choices. The Sun's heat also releases a huge quantity of carbon, striking the Earth everyday with deadly, ultraviolet rays. The ozone protects us with these ultraviolet rays, but it is not enough to handle our 'solar anger'.

Xing: So, Professor! Do we have any way to save our Earth and ourselves? Why is all of this happening now? According to the Bible, in future, our lives will be full of happiness, our human body will live forever without dying; forever on this planet Earth . . . and more, as the Bible continues its message.

Olivia: Humans would still have to learn to survive without touching any natural resource of energy. Sapiens are smarter than our previous generations because they have technology today.

Humans have machines and infrastructures, but still they aren't capable enough to stop this carbon emission. It's a great story, even after human advancement, as they're still surviving on natural resources such as coal, oil, and gases. We aren't supposed to touch them at all.

Xing: Professor! Please explain my dilemma. At one place we call ourselves intelligent and on the other hand, we still haven't learned to be as electric. Is it not the failure of mankind? When would we be able to call ourselves an intelligent species?

Olivia: We can call ourselves intelligent in the future when we will have a complete electric homo sapiens life. Until we get to this point, we can't do anything to save our planet.

Xing: Professor! Electric?

Olivia: Electronic means 'survival without natural resources', but just using solar energy. Earth has come a long way and its multitudes have constantly been changing from the last 200k years.

In the last 150 years of revolutionary changes in machines and in the 60 years of technological advancement, set a new mile stone among humans.

Jimmy: Just imagine if we meet some advanced species in the future, what would you say who you are, and what are your achievements as homo sapiens? Are you still burning coal, gas, and oil, or an intelligent electric human?

Olivia: In 1964 AD, a soviet astronomer, whose name was Nikolai Kardashev, produced a hypothetical scale to use to measure a potential civilization based on the amount of energy that civilization can produce, which is today called, the Kardashev scale.

This scale is actually having 3 traditional types. Type-I is referred to as 'Planetary Civilization', requiring at least 10 to the power 16 watts of energy every year. Type-II civilization is called, 'Stellar Civilization', in which civilization creates a megastructure around the host star. They will control and live in them. Humans on Earth have found some intergalactic megastructures through advanced telescopes, but the government doesn't have the courage to unveil them.

Kardashev Type-III civilization is called, 'Galactic Civilization'. In this civilization, humans can control the total energy of its host galaxy. After so many years, we haven't found any evidence to support this theory.

There is place in the universe called 'Boots Void', which is about 330 million light years across. This patch of sky is empty. Some scientists on Earth believe that there's over 2000 galaxies.

So far, we have found 60 galaxies in that patch, but still lots of space is empty, which left a doubt about an intelligent life. But again, it's just a theory, humans don't have any evidence for A Type-III civilization.

Our present civilization is not even in Type I category. Presently, a world power consumption is about 17.35 TW (terawatts), or when you plug in this huge number into P and crackling out the numbers are on a Kardashev scale, as a civilization which will be approximately that type to 0.72, such as a civilization that already has its footsteps on the Moon. Scientists on Earth believe that, in the mid-22nd century, we will be completely electronic, and qualify under the Type-I program.

Type: Neutral

To maintain an ozone atmosphere and life, mother nature needed some important ingredients. In any perfect recipe, we need some important ingredients which we mix together and get a final dish. The same way let's imagine we are making some pasta salad.

First, we boil some pasta, cut some vegetables, and at the end we mix boiled pasta with the vegetables, and pasta sauce. The same rule goes with life-giving ingredients (molecules) as well.

These life-giving ingredients majorly include carbon, oxygen, hydrogen, and nitrogen. The ratio for every component and their perfect combination decides the life on Earth and anywhere else in the Universe.

Yet, Earth is a unique planet because we haven't found any life anywhere else in the universe. The unique thing about Earth is its law of accounting. For example, in accounting, we balance receivables and payables equally at the end of year.

On Earth, living plants and animals exchange and take several living molecules from nature which they will have to return back to nature when they die. This maintains our balances of our lives. We exchange oxygen and carbon-dioxide from trees. Trees release oxygen and in return inhale carbon-dioxide. Carbon particles are hotter than any other molecule and makes the atmosphere warm and hot.

The Earth absorbs a sufficient quantity of carbon from the Sun every day, and excess carbon usually returns (reflect) back to the empty space in different directions in the solar system. Life really needed carbon molecules in a perfect quantity to survive.

Daphne: Professor! This means, less carbon will freeze this world, and more will warm the planet.

Olivia: Absolutely, that's what's in the news today in the twenty-first century, which is popular as 'Global Warming'; 'agenda for debate'. Extra heat is burning life-giving oxygen, and hydrogen (H 2O) atoms apart from each other.

Ice on the arctic cap is melting every year on a gradual scale. Some of the most dominant scientists say, that by the end of the twenty-first century, this ice cap will be completely wiped out of the surface. The cap represents a balance sheet of our atmosphere and shows a positive feedback, if it exists.

Xing: So, why are we facing this global warming? Are we responsible for this mis happening, or somebody else? Is there anything we can do to save ourselves?

Olivia: Global warming may be a new topic for human discussions today, but it started affecting our atmosphere millions of years ago.

This was the time when the atmosphere was mostly filled with oxygen. About 250 million years ago this ice cap was mostly covered down to Los Angeles today, and since this time, uncovering our planet and barely left on top.

Every vehicle, machinery, Aero plane, or even humans and other living animals exhale multiple carbon molecules a day which adds up to the atmosphere. When this environment was being made up, it was supposed to be for humans and other living animals.

Jimmy: God didn't know that humans will reshape this planet with their intelligence. When humans realized this intelligence, the very first thing he demanded, was luxury. In a nutshell, less work, and more output.

This intelligence made humans as a criminal. They started cheating with nature. Cheating with accounting laws, made by nature, cost humans as a global warming. But, our cheating is still a tiny contribution to this environment.

On the other side, trees are also responsible for taking (inhaling) this excess deadly carbon-dioxide from the atmosphere. In selfishness, humans are also chopping down the trees day by day for their furniture and housing needs. Right now, there is nothing humans can do about it. Human life will affect, one way or another.

BERT: In a manner of speaking, nature is angry with humans because they think they are smart and extract all-natural deposits, such as oil and gases, which they return in cheaper carbon form. Nature doesn't need this additional poisoner in a quantity of carbon.

Xing: Professor! I am really worried now, and carbon atom seems to be a nightmare. Can't we make an anti-carbon molecule with the help of science and try to reduce some heat off of our planet?

Olivia: Oh Xing! Carbon molecule is not that bad. After reacting evil, carbon doesn't just have a downside. It also has an angel, miraculous face which make you and me alive to this moment.

Xing: Angel! Really?

Olivia: About 13.5 billion years ago when the big bang happened, it released billions of trillions of subatomic particles. These subatomic particles had a wide variety of dust and gases, such as hydrogen, oxygen, carbon, nitrogen, helium, sulphuric acid, and many more.

When the universe was crowning one of its creation, out of many atoms, carbon atoms got the supreme power. We cannot make any matter without a carbon particle in it. This love of carbon attracted and started forming bigger and bigger shapes. Eventually these shapes started forming the stars, planets, moons, galaxies, and other objects in the Universe.

The Time Machine : Homo Sapiens Version

Jimmy: Carbon is the only element in this entire universe which bound other elements together. We can take an example of our English alphabet, from A to Z, as different elements around us, including oxygen, carbon, hydrogen, and nitrogen. These letters are nothing if we see them apart. We can't use them in language, neither will anyone understand it completely, even after our facial expression.

So, for a better communication, we have to connect these letters to different words, and eventually complete sentences. More letters lead to a bigger sentence. Imagine that the English language gave all its power to the alphabet 'C'. Now people have to make all their words and sentences with the letter 'C'. They can't imagine even a word or sentence without a letter 'C' in it.

Olivia: The bigger the shape we see around, for example, like a table, chair, roof, trees, sun, planets, trees, or even the human body are hard to imagine without a carbon atom. Carbon helps make other elements bind together so that they can make a different shape, such as a living, or a non-living object. Different shapes take different quantities of carbons, and different combinations of elements to work together, for a perfect shape.

Our human body is no exception, with 65% of oxygen atoms and nearly 18% carbon atoms to work together, so that we can call us alive. Modern humans call it carbohydrates to cover up their daily needs for carbon in their hairless body.

Xing: Our body has a perfect combination of different atoms and molecules. But what about our nature and atmosphere? Or, what if they interchange their ratios of quantity? While repositioning the ratios, would life still be able to survive on Earth, allowing our planet to be stable?

Olivia: Any mismatch of the combination of these atoms could destabilize the concept of life. Nothing can survive under these conditions. It doesn't matter if you live on the land, ocean, or fly in the sky. Anything and everything shall die in those deadly circumstances.

Xing: Professor! Was it happening to us before?

Olivia: Actually, it happened to us in the past around 300 million years ago.

BERT! Please take us to a world when it was all starting.

Time Machine Power : On

Time Set to : 300 Million Years

Type : Past

Olivia: This place is similar to home, this looks like Earth, having difficulty finding our own continent. Earth was so different back then. Constellation of stars were different as well. How are we going to recognize our planet? Our time machine is traveling about 350 million years back in time. There were no continents but a huge one super continent and one giant ocean.

Our Earth has just celebrated its 4 billionth year old anniversary and opened the door for land-life. So far life was breathing, just under water and the land was empty without life. There were no flowers, animals, or even birds. Dinosaurs wouldn't yet be evolved for another 90 million years in the future. Let's examine what's going on here. The air feels so different out here. Our meter shows a strange result which is installed on an outside wall of this time machine. The atmosphere has more oxygen in the entire Earth's history before, or until, the twenty-first century in the future.

BERT: We're presently traveling in the carboniferous period and there's a 'Meter alert!'; the atmosphere had almost twice the oxygen as of today.

Xing: Professor! Why was there so much oxygen back then?

Olivia: About 320 million years ago a miracle happened. A new kind of life evolved.

Daphne: What kind of life is this that can produce oxygen in such huge amounts, changing the Earth's atmosphere so dramatically?

Olivia: If you look at the Earth from a little further distance, some parts appear to be colourful. The ocean from above looks blue, the sub-Saharan desert, yellow, and the jungle and provincial parks, green. Presently, its less green, but most of the Earth appeared green before. In the twenty-first century, human's greed put themselves into a compulsion of destroying trees to construct their homes and other necessities.

Trees are like little plants; they breathe and have a wonderful chemistry inside. A tree has a deep connection with sunlight. The green texture is representative of the energy molecule. Green leaves have many factories and organic batteries, consuming energy from the sunlight, taking water from the ground, and growing taller with the help of lignin.

Previously, trees were very small because if they grew taller, gravity would cause them to fall down to the ground. Eventually a plant molecule evolved that was very strong and flexible, a particle that could support a lot of weight, as well as bend in the wind without breaking. This Lignin made it possible for trees to grow taller. Now life could climb upwards and the Earth appears to be a planet of the trees.

The Law of Nature says, whatever we borrow from it, we shall return it back in respect, once we die. So, with the same rule, trees are bound to return the entire carbon they consume all its life.

3.5 million years ago, trees were establishing their kingdom on this land, bacteria and fungi scrolled up to have a meal from a dead tree. But they couldn't do it. Again, with the law of nature, bacteria couldn't swallow the dead trees. Termites wouldn't be evolved for another hundreds of years in the future. A 'tree' takes in carbon-do-oxide, water, and sunlight to turn them into energy-rich organic matter. Then it gives off oxygen as a waste product. That's what trees and plants still do.

Xing: Apology, Professor! But you just said, we have to return everything back to nature. So, if bacteria and fungi aren't making trees to return its carbon to nature, what to do with all these dead trees? How could we return any important molecules back to nature?

Olivia: Xing! We will not return anything. Fungi and Bacteria will take another 80 million years to consume this biochemical means as lignin.

In the meantime, trees are keep on springing up, dying, falling over, and getting entombed by the sludge that builds up over the course of millions of years.

Eventually, there are going to be hundreds of billions of trees buried deep inside all over the Earth in next 80 million years until bacteria gains its immunity. It reverses the nature's rule of transaction when a plant dies and decays. The organic matter in a dead tree combines with oxygen and decomposes, putting carbon-di-oxide back into the air. This balances the books of accounting on Earth.

So, this is what happened about 300 million years ago. These trees were buried in the layer of the Earth's crust without even being eaten by bacteria's and fungi. All these trees were buried without returning carbon which belonged to the nature.

A few million years later in Siberia, a super volcano erupted, lasting hundreds of thousands of years. A tremendous quantity of carbon-dioxide came pouring out of the never-stopping volcano. This greenhouse gas drastically warmed the planet. About fifty-million years ago when thousands of millions of trees were entombed in the Earth's crust, they were turned into coal over time. Hot lava from the volcano producing this coal, creating methane, and sulfur-rich gases out of the surface.

This coal smoke made the Earth's atmosphere difficult, such as in breathing in a lot of the smoke. With months and years of frigid cold, almost each kind of life died in immorality to follow mother nature's rule.

The ratios of the atmosphere were drastically affected, and 99.99% of life completely vanished on the Earth's surface. Only bacteria managed to survive, having kicked back almost all forms of life on Earth. It took a few hundred thousand years to life to bounce back.

In the twenty-first century A.D., humans have now built multiple mines around the globe. They extract all these deposits in the form of coal, gases, minerals, and oils after 300 million years later.

BERT: Professor! Time change!

Olivia: This time, the gods have a different plan for life. Nobody knew, but the Earth is going to be run by some powerful creatures as life is back again. Previously, changes in combination of atmospheric composition, was the major reason for these creatures to end its extinction, opening the door for 'human life'.

We have probably heard about the phrase 'Survival of the Fittest'. In the modern world, corporate workers often play this game at work. But other than that, is there any true example?

Once upon a time, there was a kingdom on our own planet Earth. The rulers were cruel, killing many innocent people. Subjects, including our ancestors, were threatened everywhere.

Xing: We are still here, meaning, rulers have gone and now we are dominating this planet. But what exactly are we referring to about, and how long back? Who were these incapable ancestors? Who were the rulers?

Olivia: About 65 million years ago, Dinosaurs had their long run on the kingdom on our planet Earth. Yes, 'Dinosaurs', we all have heard about these creatures.

Daphne: When and where were they? Might we assume they were only a few or many? If they were here, where have they gone now? People say that it's just a fictional propaganda and a fantasy.

Olivia: With the help of archeological evidences, humans have finally got some answers. Let's buckle up and find out what happened back then.

While we are travelling back in the past, I would like to assure you that we are an invisible object, safe from the outside world, which is going to vanish in few minutes. We are here to see the "Cicxulub Impact" on our own planet.

About 65 million years ago, the Earth was leading by some gigantic monsters. These killing creatures ruled our planet for almost 160 million years. Humans have been living here for only 300 thousand years, so we can assume how developed, intelligent, and wild were they.

Like today, we're surrounded by multiple dog breeds, Dinosaurs were also in enormous number and in multiple breeds as well. Some of them were vegetarians, while others were depended on other smaller animals. Archeologists and biologists would probably never be certain about the Dinosaurs accurate sizes because most of them completely burned and were buried deep in the earth; Recovering impressions of skin, complete skeletons, and soft tissues, however, give us an approximate figure.

Thirty-nine feet tall and 74 feet long, the "Giraffatitan branch" of Dinosaurs were the tallest and heaviest animals at that time, and they have been the biggest ground animal in Earth's 4.5 billion years of history. Their weight was around 50,000 to 60,000 kilograms. We humans found a complete skeleton of this gigantic predator in 1907 that is currently mounted in the Berlin Museum. While the smallest herbivorous dinosaurs breed included *Microceratus* and *Wannanosaurus*, they were about 60 cm (2 feet) long each.

Time Machine Power : On

Time : 65 Million Years

Direction : Past

Place: Gulf of Mexico

We are here now, just hours away from the Chicxclub impact. A 180 kilometres wide asteroid is about to hit our Earth. We are going to witness the biggest Tsunami, Super Earthquake, volcanic eruption, and acid rain in the entire history of the Earth. This wide rock had smashed through the Earth and the crust was badly broken. In a few days, the Earth's atmosphere was completely covered with the carbon molecules and filled with the hot atoms. Hot lava smoke created a black cloud all over the globe. The shockwaves created ultimate radio waves, killing almost all the birds and ground animals in a few hours around the American continent.

BERT: Captain! Time to take off.

Olivia: The ozone is our only shield and we shall protect it in God's will. He created us with an intelligent mind to understand nature's rule and power. We may not be able to do anything in the twenty-first century, but the twenty-second century would probably have a new dawn of electronic life. By this time, humans shall have a complete understanding of nature's kingdom.

❏

Destination E
Beginning of Science

Jimmy: While humanity was taken over by religion and global warming, still, it kept a continuous effect on Earth. Even after accepting religion, Gods were never showed up amongst humanity, but instead sent messages as revelations, vision, or a dream. According to sacred scriptures, the Gods have sometimes sent their avatars in the past as well. But the real question is, are they coming to save us now from unstable solar storms and the continuous warming up of the planet?

BERT: Neutral mode active!

Olivia: We humans have one special thing which lies inside us: "Curiosity". The curiosity to know everything which is beyond our sight and approach. Yes, we are curious to know, for the things that are strange, and far away. Humans have been working towards these imaginations for centuries.

Our extraordinary journey has actually started in the early seventeenth century, when Galileo invented a telescope. By far, human life is quite simple to measure, and stars were the only digital calendar available at this time. This telescopic view in 1609 A.D. allowed us to see far beyond imagination.

The telescope was initially invented by Hans Lippershey in 1608 A.D., but Galileo added some expensive parts from England, completing a true copy of a telescope in 1609 A.D.

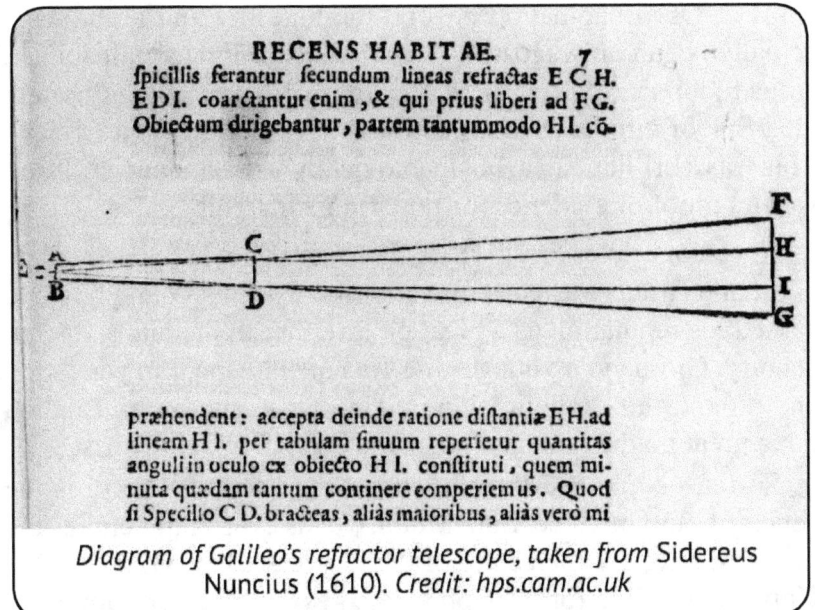

RECENS HABITAE. 7

fpicillis ferantur fecundum lineas refractas E C H.
E D I. coarctantur enim, & qui prius liberi ad F G.
Obiectum dirigebantur, partem tantummodo H I. cō-

præhendent: accepta deinde ratione diftantiæ E H. ad
lineam H I. per tabulam finuum reperietur quantitas
anguli in oculo cx obiecto H I. conftituti, quem mi-
nuta quædam tantum continere comperiemus. Quod
fi Specilio C D. bracteas, alias maioribus, alias verò mi

Diagram of Galileo's refractor telescope, taken from Sidereus Nuncius (1610). *Credit: hps.cam.ac.uk*

Xing: Captain! Apology, but why is this newly invented telescope so special? What can it see that we don't with the naked eye?

Jimmy: Human eyes are strong enough and evolved to see long distances on Earth and beyond. However, the human eye itself, is a unique organ, and sculpted even before humans were evolved on the planet.

Human eyes have a phenomenal lens system which adjusts its size according to the light we see. With 556 mega pixel camera vision, our eyes can see far distant objects where ordinary cameras give up.

Even with this kind of advanced feature, our eyes aren't capable to see everything in this Universe. Galileo's telescope accepted our precious wish and gave us a power to see deep inside the universe.

Right after Galileo's incredible invention, Uranus, Neptune and Pluto' have been found in our outer most solar system, which were unknown to our ancestors. Rigveda, Surya Siddhanta, Old and New Testaments, have only references for six planets.

Olivia: Our imagination beyond the blue sky and night stars, actually began on August 11, 1451, AD. A German philosopher, an astronomer referred to as Nicholas of Cusa, gave a perfect idea-link of infinite space which was very unique to the society. This was a brilliant idea, but theologically was challenged. There was no proof or evidence to support this incredible idea.

A century later in 1548 A.D., a miracle happened when Giordano Bruno was born in northern Italy. This young boy had earned his reputation as a great philosopher in the late sixteenth century. Giordano's younger life was mostly spent in education and around the Catholic church. He just wasn't a philosopher, but a great mathematician, poet, and cosmological theorist.

So far, people and the church believed that the Earth is the center of our Universe; Sun, Moon, Venus everything circles the Earth, and we are the center of the Universe. Everything in this Universe is made for us. God created everything for humans to enjoy and there is nothing else important.

It is 1590 A.D. and Giordano has started observing the night stars, constellations, and planetary movements. Giordano wasn't a scientist because science didn't exist at this time, but this could be a time when science was just being born among humans.

He has calculated that the Earth is not the center of our solar system, but the Sun is. Along with the Moon and other six planets, Earth circle's the Sun and the our planet is not important at all, but the Sun.

It is 1592 A.D. and Giordano is now against the Roman Catholic's belief that Earth is the center of the Universe. Other sources, such as Rigveda from Hinduism (Sanatan), Jewish scriptures, Quran, and Buddhist scriptures, are also reiterating the identical aspect as is the church.

Type: Past

Time: 1593 AD

Place: Rome, Italy

It's 1593 and he was tried for heresy by the Roman inquisition on charges including denial of several core Catholic doctrines, including eternal damnation, Trinity, the divinity of Christ, the virginity of Mary, and transubstantiation.

Court Judge: Prisoner! Do you have anything to say concerning your guilt by going against the church's belief?

Giordano: Your Honour! Pardon me! But what is my guilt? I'm not against Christ, church, or the Bible. I had a vision that our Universe is infinite, and the Earth is not the center. The night stars are just the other Sun's and Earth's, and the Moon's circle them.

Court Judge: But the Bible says something else. Going against Christianity and the church will cost you your life. If you don't stop now, you will either be hanged or burned alive in the name of Jesus Christ. This court is adjourned until the next date!

Type: Neutral

Olivia: It was unfortunate, but after a year, the Catholic church sent him for a lifetime of imprisonment. On February 17, 1600 A.D., he was burned alive in front of the Catholic church in Rome.

Nine years later, in 1609 A.D. when Galileo looked through his telescope for the very first time, he saw the Saturn rings, Mars' great canyon, the Moon, and other planetary motions. With this telescope, we understood that the Sun is the center, not us. Other planets and the Moons constantly orbit the Sun for survival.

It was a lucky guess, but Giordano couldn't prove everything. This is why we are human. We cannot believe anything without a solid evidence.

So, Galileo set these convex and concave lenses at a proper distance in a tube, adding a collecting space in between the lenses. Now, we could collect lights from far distant stars which were previously invisible to human eyes.

Since then, we have been trying to enhance the telescope's power and its visual sight with some other technological advancement. This collecting space in between the lenses became wider and bigger over the time. After Galileo's death, humans have been increasing its size to capture increasingly more light from distant worlds.

Now, at least humans have something in their hands to look further away from their sight. There were many improvements, and value, in addition to this telescope after Galileo's death until the late nineteenth century.

After 300 years of the non-stop journey of telescopic improvements, one thing became very clear to visualize far distant objects in the night sky, in that the telescope needs a bigger focal lens and collecting space.

BERT: The first revolutionary telescopic value enhancement took place in the late nineteenth century.

Time: 1892

Place: California, USA

Olivia: Industrialist, George Ellery Hale, was another soul in human shape who was born and brought up with curiosities. His father and grandfather had multiples of industries. George was young and had just come back home after completing his university degree. He thinks differently now and returned back with a plan which can change everything.

He arrived this morning and is trying to set up his telescope at different angles at his back yard. But he failed to visualize anything in space properly. After many tries he thought, what if he can go a little bit higher at some place; that might work. Then, he decided to go on Mount Wilson, which is located in California today.

5700 feet above the sea level, he had a substantially better clear of clearer images in his telescope, which were barely visible from his backyard. There were no clouds to cloud his vision in seeing indefinitely beyond the Earth's horizon. After this moment, he decided to build a giant telescope with a much larger collecting space that was ever built by human hands.

Eventually, in 1908 A.D., his project was completed and named as the 'Hooker telescope'. With a 2.5 meters wide focal lens, it allowed him to see greater distant objects, which was a question for the initial telescope built by Galileo.

Until 1949, Hooker's telescope was flagged as the biggest telescope on Earth, making several great discoveries over the time. In 1923, scientist Edwin Hubble, discovered our neighbour spiral galaxy 'Andromeda'. In 1929, this telescope has also discovered that our universe is expanding, and the existence of the 'dark matter' in space.

The journey from Galileo's Telescope to the Hooker's telescope, helped pave our way to different galaxies. Now, we know we have more galaxies in the universe other than our own Milky Way galaxy. This clue led us to make more powerful and advanced telescopes for mankind. In 2009, we had completely reshaped the masterpiece given by Galileo as a 'Hubble Telescope'.

The Hubble Telescope has proven to be the most advanced and powerful telescope in the entire history of mankind. This telescope is located at the Earth's upper atmosphere, which is pro in taking digital HD images from far distant objects.

Instead of placing the telescope on the Earth, we placed it in space for distant images. Then, with the help of a satellite, it transmits back the picture (data) to the Earth's surface. Humans can see how stars, planets, and galaxies are formed. Naked homo sapiens breed can actually locate the place where exactly the big bang happened.

Type: Neutral

Olivia: It's a dream to be lost in these beautiful places in the deep universe, the nebulas; how colorful they are. Traveling in the universe is beyond imagination, as everything is so far away.

Imaginations are fine, but actual work on the ground level has some limitations, even for exploration.

Space exploration is not easy as everything is so far away, and it also needs billions of dollars. And to travel far away, you need more and reliable fuel, let's say if it's a twenty years of journey with the speed of light, then you probably could reach one of Sun's neighboring stars.

The Hubble telescope gives us power to see those stars in HD quality to zoom in for close details without even going there. This telescope began a new visual journey for mankind in making themselves wonder, and include them, in cosmic calculation.

Daphne: Pardon me, Professor! But why did it become so important to know what is hidden behind those night stars?

Olivia: Excellent question, Daphne!

.........Let's take an example of the Earth, our own planet. It has soil for agriculture, water, organics, bio-chemicals, rocks, and most importantly, carbon molecules.

Our Earth isn't the only home for these molecules, but these atoms are also available everywhere in the universe. All those stars, planets, and moons are made of the same combination as the atoms.

Indeed, this is the reason we may have some sort of connection with other visible and invisible elements in the universe. These elements can be found anywhere in our solar system, as well as in the entire universe. There is a huge possibility that most, or all of these elements are connected to each other, and needing each other for survival is a real requirement in that.

Xing: May I, Professor? How could we say, without even going anywhere, to claim, which is made up of what thing?

Olivia: There is a technique which scientists used to calculate different distances and even the composition of the objects from different worlds. Light may be visible as one light sometimes, but it contains a complete spectrum, like rainbow light. It's a universal law, that blue light has a shorter wavelength, whereas red has the longest.

Apart from blue and red, there is one more kind of light which lives inside the light, that often carries heat, wherein its wavelength is longer than the red one. William Herschel was the first man to detect this unseen presence staged just below the red end of the spectrum. That's why it came to be called, infrared. Infra is Latin for the word 'below'. It's invisible, and our eyes are not sensitive to this kind of light, but the human skin, i.e. as all life is, can feel heat from this light.

Now, humans have one more light technology which could help them see even further distant objects. This infrared vision in the Hubble telescope added a supreme power of visionary.

When light travels through infinite space, it carries all colors of the spectrum with it. It doesn't matter what color you are, but everyone has to follow the same speed at this part of journey.

Alien lights from stars reaches the Earth, then humans see them with a prism. Once light strikes the prism, the spectrum lights slow down so that we can watch them dancing. Violet light, which is carried by the shortest waves we see, slows down more than red light, which has the longest waves. When scientists see these wavelengths, they find some dark spots in between the wavelengths. So, this became clearer if they were to solve this secret code.

BERT: Camera rotating to an atomic level.

Olivia: On Earth, we found that each thing has a chemical composition. Humans, animals, plants, and even the Earth itself is made by certain ratios of some molecules.

Different molecules have different atomic structures. Let's take an example of 'hydrogen' atoms, which are almost everywhere, having only one electron and one proton. In an atom, an electron doesn't exist between orbitals. It disappears from one orbital, reappearing in another.

All the elements are different from each other and recognize its persona by how electrons move inside it. The chemistry of anything is determined by its electron orbits.

There is a force which electrons dance around, but this is just an attraction, not gravity. Electrons orbit in a wavy way to the central nucleus, leaving a quantum leap in between. When the energy of the electron run, and it drops to a lower orbital, the light wave emitted, scatters.

Leaps leave an atomic light wave impression of its chemical composition which analyze that what is star made of. This was an absolute award for mankind to observe light waves from distant stars and look at them through a prism and magnify them, in order get the object's material composition.

". . . I looked again and saw God's throne;
The angels might and strength to roam
Where mortal man can face all fear,
And find life's joy on Earth is dear.

"To help and guide one on his way;
To be a friend in heart to stay.
I merely was the first of man,
Within God's wondrous grace and Plan!

❏

Destination F
Birth of Earth

Time: 4.5 Billion years

Type: Past

BERT: Captain! The Sun is very small, and we don't have enough heat to survive here, 4.5 billion years back in time. Should I turn on auto thruster?

Olivia: Yes, do it! The Universe is filled with stars and every star has its own light, energy, and the solar system. A solar system contains usually a mother star, and hundreds of billions of other smaller and bigger objects, which orbit its home star constantly, since its birth.

Xing: Professor! Do we also have a mother star?

Olivia: Yes! Our only star is the Sun. The Sun stands tall in the center of our solar system and everything else in the solar system, circles the Sun on a set, orbital pattern.

Our home star makes trillions of tons of energy to feed all these eight planets; five dwarf planets, and dozens of moons every day, every second. It also nurtures millions of other asteroids and comets in our solar system.

All these planets, moons, and asteroids are actually bounded with the Sun's gravity. The closest object, like the planet

Mercury, completes an orbit around the Sun, in just 88 days. However, our outer most planet, 'Pluto', takes almost 250 earth years to complete one circle around the Sun.

Olivia: The journey ahead is very special as our time machine will break the boundaries and enter into the Sun. After exploring the interior of the Sun, we will fly by each and every planet, eventually storming out of our solar system, and will go to the other part of our Universe.

Xing: Professor! I am excited.

Olivia: Change neutral mode and set a travel time to the Sun.

BERT: Professor! We are approaching the Sun now and will reach it in few minutes.

Olivia: Thanks! The Law of Nature is the thumb rule of this Universe. Nothing can survive forever.

Like humans and other living creatures born and die, the Stars are born, and die as well. Newly born stars are usually smaller and eventually grow bigger and bigger over time within the vast, empty space.

A Star formation takes place in a giant cloud of dust and gas. We call this colorful cloud as 'Nebula'. A star formation starts with a couple of hydrogen atoms, growing larger in this empty space. These atoms become so hot that the nuclei fuse together deep inside the atoms.

Type: Neutral

The Sun covers about 99.80% mass of the entire solar system. Humans have been gazing at the Sun since their integrity. They have worshipped the Sun when they had no-one to pray to. Its power and science are awesome. It's too big, that millions of Earth's can fit inside it. The Sun is about 27 million degrees internal temperature, which is different from the surface temperature.

Xing: What kind of process takes place inside the Sun to fuel us on Earth?

Olivia: Solar physicists say that the Sun's surface has a sound wave. Our Sun vibrates and these sound waves ripple through the inside material. Sound waves are also sending its wave through the Earth's crust, which we tracked for our records, revealing how the Sun is actually made.

The Sun releases about ten million other sound-wave frequencies throughout the solar system, affecting other objects, including the Earth. There is a multi-layered sophisticated machine system beneath the sound waves.

Right after sound waves and its blazing surface, the next layer is where light takes thousands of years to cross its zone, and in the middle, we will find its core, which fuels the entire solar system.

Xing: What is the core made of?

Olivia: The core is mostly made of gas of super charged particles, what we call plasma. The core of the Sun is about 15 million degrees inside.

About 4.5 billion years ago, when the Sun was formed, hydrogen gas and its heart was crushed under the material above. Eventually, the temperature and pressure rose so high that Hydrogen atoms broke apart into electrons and protons, creating plasma. It's like nuclear fusion, the same atomic process inside the hydrogen bomb.

Then under tremendous pressure, protons, and the plasma fuse together, releasing photons, heat, and light. Every second photons inside the Sun are being made and generating power for humanity and life on Earth.

The Sun distributes its light evenly in the entire solar system. The energy of billions of atomic bombs is released in the core of the Sun, every second of every day from the last 4.5 billion years, constantly.

The balance of the core is so precisely balanced that the plasma coming out of the core and Sun is huge, so all the mass is pulling inwards as a gravitational pull. The Sun is trying to blow from inside and it's the best, balancing of both the parts, keeping the Sun in one piece.

Once light comes out from the core, it has to face a thick layer of radiative and convection zone. It takes them about 100k years to reach the surface. The plasma is so dense in this zone that photons have to work very hard to go out on the surface, then throughout the solar system.

Photons also bring energy particles with it, reaching the Earth's surface in about eight minutes. This light born in the core reaches us after a phenomenal journey. Once these energy particles get to the Earth's surface, every living being absorbs it directly or indirectly with some source of intake food.

Daphne: Pardon me, Professor! But what if the Sun stops sending these particles one day?

Olivia: This is true, when one day the Sun would get out of its fuel, it will vanish along with the Earth as well as the entire solar system. It is very important for humans to keep an eye on the Sun for 24 hours. If anything happens, we will be awake at least.

Jimmy: It became so important for humans to understand about the Sun; more closely for the survival of mankind. And then, in 2010, humans manufactured a spacecraft called, 'Solar Dynamic Observatory', SDO in short.

It is the most sophisticated space craft made by humans so far. SDO takes full 24 hours surveillance of the Sun. Something which was actually impossible to earlier achieve by mankind. SDO was the first digital telescope to capture and learn more about Sun.

When we first looked through SDO, humans found giant tornados hundreds and thousands of miles above the surface of the Sun that could easily engulf the whole Earth. We can see all the details now and learn more about solar physics.

The best thing with this probe that we can see a range of wave length that can tell us more about solar temperature, glowing 10,000 degrees Fahrenheit. In this glow, the Sun looks featureless. But at hotter wavelengths, a far more dynamic image can be captured.

The solar storm on February 15, 2011, is the perfect example. SDO captured a CME wave; Corona mass ejection. It carried a billion of tons of plasma to destroy whatever comes on its way. Due to the Earth's magnetic field and a thick layer of ozone, we were able to survive this time, but we wouldn't always be this fortunate.

In 2003 A.D., it actually affected humans on Earth. We didn't have SDO at this time to observe closely, but we had other telescopes. In February 2003, the Sun blasted a title wave with super-heated charged particles at the speed of up to 600 million miles per hour, one of the largest solar storms ever recorded, which was aimed at Earth. Communication systems, including the Internet, were all shut down, but again, in a few months, humans started building up its loss.

The Sun controls all aspects of our lives; climate, food, and our bodies. We actually live inside the Sun's atmosphere, along with other planets. The Sun produces all the heat and light for our survival. If we had no Sun, then the life would be funny to amaze.

BERT: Professor! Our heating sensors are alerting red. We shall move quickly!

Jimmy: Put it on Neutral and set the time for Planet Mercury. And before we go any further, we should have a little understanding of how big our solar system is.

The Sun is a star which holds a massive gravity in its core and shines in the middle of our solar system, which is about 9.5 billion kilometers (100 AU) across in diameter.

Olivia: In the twenty-first century, humans would actually use a term to understand distances within our solar system as 'Astronomical Unit'. The Earth is exactly 149.6 million kilometers away from our Sun and we use this distance as our yardstick as '1 Astronomical Unit'. The Sun sends its light and energy all across the solar disc - up to the 50 AU.

We can divide our solar system in 2 separate parts, inner solar system, and outer solar system. The inner solar system has those objects which are orbiting the Sun closely and faster. Whereas the outer most objects go slowly and have a bigger orbital path around the Sun.

The inner solar system contains four rocky planets, including Mercury, Venus, Earth, and Mars. The outer solar system contains four gassy planets, including Jupiter, Saturn, Uranus, and Neptune.

There is huge gap in between Mars and Jupiter's orbital path, which is also known to be a border line in between the two systems. In this wide gap, there is a huge belt of asteroids which are also bound with the Sun's gravity, orbiting around the Sun since the birth of our solar system.

Right after Neptune's orbital path to the end of our solar system, there is one more belt known as the Kuiper belt. The Kuiper belt is wider and almost twenty times bigger than the inner asteroid belt. This belt is a home for trillions of comets which were neglected and pushed away to the outer most solar system during the solar birth.

An asteroid's composition and structure are completely different from a comet. An asteroid is mostly made of minerals, organics, and water particles from the dust cloud when our Sun was being born.

Comets are mostly containing hydrogen, carbon, and ice in its structure. Comets and asteroids are the object which couldn't take any shape in all these years, now circling the Sun as orphans.

BERT: Approaching planet Mercury in 20 seconds.

Olivia: Mercury is the smallest and the innermost planet of our solar system. It orbits the Sun completely in just 88 days. It's named after a Roman God. Mercury, 'the messenger to God', has one similar thing as the Earth, which is a magnetic field, while Venus and Mars have in lower grade.

0.4 AU far from the Sun, this angry planet has two faces. Like our Earth rotates completely just in 24 hours, but Mercury rotates on its position in 59 earth days.

On Earth, we get light during the day time and get some extra time to cool our surface during night. This night and day system keeps us alive.

After facing a tremendous heat, this planet is oppositely uniquely different. The slow rotation on planet Mercury makes the front as the bright side - about 427 degrees Celsius, but the other half, as cold as minus 173 degrees Celsius.

Human explorers made a probe named, 'MESSENGER', to observe and take close images of Mercury.

You might think it would be easy to travel to Mercury, which is relatively close to Earth, but it's very hard to put a spacecraft in orbit at a small planet located so close to the massive gravity of the Sun.

In order to get there, Messenger performed 6 different flybys during August 2, 2005 to September 29, 2009. This probe collected and produced enough images for a complete global map of Mercury. The Messenger's mission finally ended April 30, 2015, because it ran out of fuel, crashing onto Mercury's surface.

BERT: Approaching planet Venus in 20 seconds.

Olivia: Venus, the second orbital object from the Sun is named after a Roman Goddess of love and beauty from Holy Scriptures. Venus and Earth are almost similar in size, mass, density, composition, and gravity. Venus is mostly covered by a thick and rapidly spinning atmosphere.

Xing: Sorry Professor! But I have heard some rumors about life migrated from Venus due to global warming effect, long time ago. Due to the Sun's growing size, may it be possible that Venus ever supported life, and they migrated to Earth?

Olivia: Xing! Venus's atmosphere is too hot to support human or any kind of life in today's condition. But it is possible that once life had survived on the Venusian ground, as we found a few water traces. Venus is affected by the greenhouse gas effect today. In this effect heavy particles in clouds trap the sunlight and never leave the atmosphere, which makes it hotter and hotter.

Its atmosphere consists mainly of carbon dioxide with clouds of sulphuric acid droplets. The surface temperature recorded higher than 470 degrees; almost 10 times greater than Earth's surface.

Venus completes a full circle around the Sun in just 225 Earth days. Venus's day is about 117 Earth days long. Humans have sent a probe (spacecraft/camera), which landed on Venusian ground, and survived only a few hours before being destroyed by the tremendous heat in the atmosphere.

BERT: Venusian flyby is ending in 10 seconds. Approaching Home!

Olivia: Except for a few water traces, we have never found any trace of life on Venusian ground, but we can say this planet, right here, is our only home, Earth. With one Moon, Earth orbits the Sun at the third place - from the center in habitable zone.

This zone is a perfect distance from its home star that water on the planet is neither frozen nor hot enough to evaporate, instead staying in liquid form. Earth is at the perfect distance from the Sun so that water can stay in liquid form.

Liquid water helps life to exist. Without a water particle, biology cannot perform. Any biological structure, including humans, birds, animals, flowers, trees or even bacteria, cannot exist in absence of this life-giving molecule.

Our solar system contains a home star (Sun), 8 planets, 5 dwarf planets, dozens of moons, millions of asteroids, and trillions of comets. The Sun is the only parent, and all other objects are like children. The Sun feeds them with light and energy particles, and in return they circle the Sun all their lives.

As our parents give birth to us and our birth has taken place because of our parents, the same rule goes to our solar system.

BERT! Set time to birth of Earth, we will stay here for a while then we will head out towards Mars.

BERT: Roger that Professor!

Time: 4.567 Billion Years ago
Place: Unknown Nebula

Olivia: When and how exactly, was the Earth born? Humans have been researching and looking for these answers for centuries. It was a mysterious task for historians and other geologists to figure out the true age of the Earth. In the twentieth century, humans started looking for the oldest rocks on our planet.

Daphne: This perfectly make sense! The oldest rocks may have some clues that can help to determine the age of Earth.

BERT: There are no such rocks existing from that time. Continuous volcanic eruption, and tectonic forces, including continental shifts, destroyed all the evidences and clues.

Type: Neutral

Olivia: In 1956, the great geochemist, Clair Cameron Patterson, collected some meteorite samples at à Meteor crater on a desert landscape of Northern Arizona. This giant hole in the ground is formed when a massive meteor slammed into the earth a long time ago.

Meteoroids were formed from the exact mineral dust cloud as the Earth during the birth of the Sun. Some of them are still roaming around the Sun, often falling onto Earth. Our thick ozone layer burns these rocks completely prior to touching the ground. But some meteorites often survive, and we can find them on ground.

Young Patterson took all these samples to his research laboratory for a contamination-free experimental process. Results were astonishing and revealed the greatest discovery in the entire human history. This meteorite sample contained minerals, metals, amino acids, and even water from the solar dust cloud, untouched since its birth. These molecules are the building blocks for life and for us today. These preserved molecules from the dust cloud dated back exactly 4.5 billion years when our Sun and Earth were being made.

About 4.5 billion years ago, the Earth was formed from a disc of gas and dust orbiting the new-born Sun. The cloud and dust later cooled down and started forming in tiny, mineral particles. Later, these particles started sticking together and formed little and medium-sized rocks.

In the course of the next few million years, these little rocks will merge together and form bigger and bigger objects, and eventually, the biggest object in what we known as Earth today.

However, there were many rocks which couldn't take any shape yet, and still are roaming around as meteoroids.

Daphne: Understandable! But what about other objects in the solar system? Were they formed in the same way as Earth was?

Olivia: Smart question, Daph! Planets and other object formations totally depends on the ratio of dust and cloud particles during star birth on that disci orbital path. So, when the Earth was being made, an orbit contained perfect conditions, that, at least the Earth can be hostile as a big mineral grain object.

The first few million years were miserable on Earth. It was a hot giant molten ball of rock orbiting Sun. Continuous bombardment of meteors made Earth difficult to contend with. But extreme cold of -450 degrees of empty space made liquid rock lava into a thin crust. In the same way we get a creamy oxidized layer on our hot milky beverage.

Daphne: Pardon me, Professor! But today, Earth is very different then from this moment what we see here, right now. What happened that this molten rock transformed into present Earth?

Olivia: Right Daph! With the low degree temperature, heavy particles on the surface sank down and formed one big iron core in the center of the Earth.

Even after a thin crust, continuous bombardment of meteoroids is in the headlines today. Every impact brought a major building block with these meteors. These meteors brought major molecules, helping life come to an existence. Water and amino acid especially played a vital role to forming biology in different shapes on Earth. The 'Geography of Earth' was actually changed because of the biology and life evolution.

Just in 30 million years, it had a 3-kilometer-thick crust with a solid, rocky land, and the ocean was full of water. It was very strange, but an unknown planet slightly hit the Earth and scratched its outer mental rock with some part of its inner iron core about 3.5 billion years ago. At this time, the Earth was very young and completely damaged. But I would say, it was a perfectly precise hit mark considered to be, good luck.

Xing: A good-luck mark?

Olivia: A good luck can be explained in two different ways. This hit transformed Earth's 3 kilometers thin crust and ocean depth to 10 kilometers thick. This wide depth of ocean helped millions of species and plants to breathe underwater.

This hit also scratched the outer rocky mental with little iron core. The debris with this impact fell into Earth's orbit and formed our Moon. The Moon was 10 times closer when it was formed. Continuous spinning of the Earth and Moon on its axis made both objects stable, pushing the Moon away to enjoy 24 hours in a day instead of 4 hours a day.

Daphne: What if the Moon isn't there? Would it affect human life on Earth?

Olivia: The Moon holds a gravity and orbit around the Earth in a manner that it spins stably on its axis. However, it shifts in few million years by a degree or so. Without the Moon, the Earth will be a randomly spinning planet which would rotate in any direction.

This drastic change will affect day and night time, extreme weather conditions wouldn't be carrying any intelligent life around. The ocean circulatory system will be shut down completely and wind wouldn't be flown.

The Moon is our souvenir and guarding our planet from the last 3.5 billion years. Any object coming towards the Earth has to face the Moon first. The Moon takes all those impacts on itself in order to save Earth. This is the reason the Moon has so many scars and craters on its surface.

Xing: Professor! I am curious to know that now we have water, land, and a stable 24 hours long day. But how did atmosphere and oxygen formed, and life evolved eventually?

Olivia: Bert, please take us to Mexico 2.6 billion years in the past.

BERT: Roger that, Captain!

Olivia: We're here. Everything looks barren. No birds, flowers, humans; nobody at all. There is no ozone or protective layer to support any kind of life. The Sun's deadly ultraviolet rays will kill you within a few seconds.

But, it was a great day when a new kind of life evolved under the shallow water, right here. These little creatures have started turning into a life-giving machine called, 'Cianobacterias'. They just take a little sunlight and water, and in return, they produce a bi-product as oxygen. The first few million years they were dominating our planet and filled our entire atmosphere with excessive, oxygen gas. The oxygen we breathe today was long ago created and filled by cyanobacteria.

About 2 billion years ago, bacteria branched off to another kind of life known after as eukaryotes. Eventually, it helped birth to other animals, plants, fungi, protozoans and even humans in the form of genetic life.

BERT: Captain! Earth flyby is ending in 20 seconds. Approaching Mars!

Olivia: Now we should get ready to leave our only home and prepare to see a completely new world called, Mars, 'the red planet'. About 1.5 AU away from the center, Mars orbits the Sun at the 4th place. Mars is about 10 times smaller than the Earth, but regardless of size, Mars has about the same land mass as Earth.

The World War for Mars began in the late '60's. The United States and the Soviet Union, two of the world's most powerful nations, are fighting over Mars. Mental cold war has already started in between these countries. In other countries, they often take part of a controversy debate for their unprecedented effort.

Apart from controversy, both nations are developed enough to understand global warming, and try to think something about it.

Both countries have the world's most intelligent engineer's team in their research facilities. This global warming effect will actually decide the existence of the future human race on our planet.

In the '60's, we don't have much technology, but the Soviet Union has recently sent a radio satellite (Sputnik 1) into the Earth's orbit in 1957 for the first time in the entire human history. It was a miraculous day when they launched a manmade piece of a small machine in the Earth's lower orbit.

Computers will not be invented for another 13 years in the future. Smart phone devices are also generations away. With no technology, engineers are working so hard in order to get some close-up pictures from Mars.

On November 28, 1964, both rivals have now only a few hours to launch for their extraordinary crafts which will reveal Mars and were able to capture some close-up images. They had completed their mission, capturing about 45 images, and transmitting back to Earth. The phenomenal camera system on these crafts were also installed with an ultraviolet spectrometer to search for methane on Mars.

Xing: Professor! That's it? Were these images and methane data in the Martian atmosphere helped us at all to understand Mars?

Olivia: You are thinking right about that; a few pictures and level of methane is not enough for any Mars exploration research. But remember, back in the '60's, humans were capable of making these crafts, and we should be proud of them for this unprecedented victory of mankind.

So far, humans have seen Mars only through a telescope. When they looked through a telescope, humans found perfect water traces (waves) all around the Mars. They also found some active volcanos and gigantic craters on the Martian surface. These pictures are amazing, confirming water marks, and a thin layer of atmosphere on the Martian surface.

These clues aided us to think about a decade or so, and NASA was able to convince the government for an extra budget of 217 million US dollars for a new 'Viking' project in the '70's. The Viking project included two different spacecraft's - Viking 1 and Viking 2.

Each craft has two major parts, one is orbiter, which will help to receive data from the probe on Martian ground and transmit back to Earth. The other part will be dropped on the surface at some safe place to dig on the Martian ground and analyze the composition of soil and minerals. It will also be used to measure the atmospheric composition of Mars.

Xing: Apology, Professor! Just for my personal notes, why is the government throwing millions and billions of dollars on these projects? What do they expect from Mars? Is there any precious metal hidden underneath the surface, or we are chasing Greek or Hindu mythology as a reference for any ancient connection with Mars?

Olivia: Mars is our neighboring planet and there is a huge possibility that Mars could contain an identical composition of life-giving elements. As the increasing size of the Sun, the Earth wouldn't be a habitable place in the future.

Jimmy: In order to save humanity, the government is trying hard to find a place. In the future, we will be more developed to make some kind of vehicle to go further away; however, Mars could buy some time as its orbit is about 0.5 AU further away from Earth.

Olivia: After the Viking mission, it's now confirmed that Mars has about a 24 hours and 40 minutes long day (SOL). We have also found ice just a few inches beneath the soil. Carbon, Nitrogen, Calcium, and other minerals on the Martian surface are plentiful. These clues are more than enough to tell us that life might have survived in the past or may support in the future.

So far, we know that the Earth is a unique planet and that the entire universe is created for us. The most unique and precious thing on the Earth is 'life'. If we find any clue which leads to a different planet or object which supports life, our uniqueness will be lost. It's very important for humans to understand that if life can be found in our neighborhood, and on planet Mars, the universe is full of life and we are not unique anymore.

About 30 years later in 2003, the Republican Party had sanctioned another budget in the assembly for one Billion dollars on the Mars Exploration program.

Humans have now decided to dig deeper if life really can survive on Mars. We have made 2 identical rovers, Spirit and Opportunity. These rovers are like a medium car sized 6-wheel robotic bodies which can be handled by humans on Earth.

Humans send them a command in the morning for the entire day. These rovers would work only in the day time and will go in sleep mode during the night. Both rovers have a big solar panel which fuels its energy. They also have a mechanical arm, driller, microscope, telescope, and infrared lights to observe and analyze better.

The government has funded this project to look for and characterize a variety of different Martian rocks and soil structures which carry clues to the past water activity. This activity process usually depends on the minerals deposited long ago in the past.

These rovers are propelled to determine the composition of minerals, soil, craters, meteorites, and rocks. This rover mission would also help humans understand about Martian geology, mineralogy, and the environmental conditions. These rovers were constructed with the ability to move and dig around for samples.

So, now we know an object (Mars) which is close enough, holding the similar composition of life, as Earth. These compositions are extremely important to support life and build a technological world with copper, and other important metals as Earth.

But, these kinds of advanced rovers were helpless on this rocky planet as they can't go to each and every rock and drill them for samples. Recently, the Democratic Party passed a budget for a new Curiosity program for 2.5 Billion dollars. This would be the last program; after this program our astronauts will go there physically for ground research.

Today is November 26, 2011 and U.S. President Barack Obama will be giving a green signal to launch in a few minutes. The Curiosity rover is the most sophisticated rover ever built by mankind. We can understand in the same way as cell phone devices.

In 2003, we had button-based phones, but we aliened them in 2011 and started using smart phones. This rover is actually a smart rover, give and take.

Curiosity's job was to look for past places on Mars that could have sustained life. We have a laser beam which could shoot at the rock then, it burns the surface and gas comes off. This gas tells us the chemical composition of this rock.

We can shoot an X-ray's light through the rocks to see how actual chemicals are held together. Curiosity also drills, and after drilling, we can separate different particle sizes down to the microns level.

After spending a few years with this machine on Mars, humans would say that the Martian land is wet, and it can sustain life. We have found hematite, which can only survive in water on the Earth. There are all of the chemical compositions that are needed to support life, that's available on the Martian surface. Mars is also covered with clouds, and some degree of moisture consists in the atmosphere.

BERT: Martian flyby is ending in 20 seconds.

Olivia: Thanks BERT!

So, passenger! We will come back here one day and terraform Mars as a habitant place.

BERT: Time set to Jupiter.

Olivia: There is a huge gap in between Mars and Jupiter which is filled with big, rocky asteroids belt. These are the rocks which couldn't take any shape during the birth of our solar system. Hot gases from the solar-dust cloud were very dense and compressed to make these objects.

Asteroids are orbiting Sun, for the same reason as we do, for 'energy' particle. An asteroid is mostly made of iron, rock, mineral, water, and precious metals. Some metallic asteroids are composed by the most expensive metals like Osmium, Nickel, Ruthenium, Iridium, Rhodium, Palladium, Platinum, Gold, and Magnesium.

Jimmy: That's right, because these asteroids carry rare elements which were composed naturally in empty vacuumed space, billions of years ago. But, this is important for mankind: to keep an eye on this Asteroid belt as if, they would leave the orbit and change their path to a different direction. Asteroids could actually change their path and can make their way to Earth in anytime.

Xing: Do we have any history with these kinds of impacts?

Olivia: It happened about 65 million years ago when an asteroid changed its way from this belt and slammed into the Earth. 80% of the life on Earth was wiped out at this time. I know it's a sad moment but if it didn't happen, we wouldn't be here. We are here at this moment; because of this asteroid so that we could evolve as intelligent creatures.

BERT: Approaching Jupiter at 500 meters.

Olivia: Jupiter orbits the Sun at the fifth place about 5.2 AU away. It is the biggest planet in the entire solar system. It has more mass than combining all other planets together. We can fit thousands of Earth, like an object inside Jupiter.

Well, Jupiter is working hard, holding all of these asteroids with its gravity so that we can live here on Earth. If, one day something happens to Jupiter, we will be lost shortly by an asteroid-hit like it happened 65 million years ago.

Jupiter was named as Zeus and plays a major role in Greek mythology. The Romans had later changed this name to 'Jupiter'. It was first seen by Galileo Galilei right after his telescope invention.

Jupiter has 69 moons in total, but out of them, four moons can be observed from the Earth on a clearer night sky. These 4 moons: Io, Europa, Ganymede, and Calisto were initially discovered by Galileo.

Xing: Galileo might be an angel. His invention has still been opening our eyes.

Olivia: That's true! About 5.2 AU away, this gassy planet is mostly made of hydrogen gas. A touch of helium makes Jupiter very angry and it triggers monster hurricanes on the surface. Scientists are observing their tornados and hurricanes from the last 300 years and they are still active. Some of them are big enough to engulf half a dozen Earth-like objects inside it.

Unlike Earth, Jupiter rotates completely on its axis just in 10 hours. It takes about 12 years to circle the Sun's orbit to this gigantic planet.

Out of many moons, Europa is the special one, as it has more water than the Earth. It may be possible that life could survive there, or that it already exists. Scientists are working so hard to dive into one of these worlds. Of course, robotically at first, then maybe manmade crafts will make their way to Europa.

BERT: Time elapse in 5 seconds, we may lose the signal.

Jimmy: Put it on Neutral Please! Hot hydrogen gas from Jupiter was killing our camera system.

Olivia: Let's proceed to Saturn.

BERT: Approaching Saturn in few seconds.

Olivia: Saturn is probably the most beautiful planet in the solar system. Its ring system is amazing. Like Jupiter, Saturn is also made up of hydrogen and helium gas. About 9.5 AU away from Sun, Saturn is the second largest planet in the solar system.

It completes a circle around the Sun in approximately every 30 years. The structure of Saturn is called as a markedly oblate spheroid, with a polar diameter some ten percent smaller than that at the equator.

The Moons of Saturn are numerous ranging in multiple sizes and structures. It took hundreds of years to decipher Saturn's ring system.

At first, when Galileo observed Saturn with his telescope, he found this phenomenal ring system, but nobody knew how it is made up of, and with what; why these rings are circling a planet.

In 1992, humans have observed these ring systems the very first time with the Voyager 1 spacecraft flyby mission. When the camera went too close to these rings, humans found this ring was made of multiple smaller moons swirling around together. It's like a marathon of thousands of car-sized moons around Saturn.

Apart from this ring system, Saturn has about 62 other moons which at least have 1 km diameter. Out of many moons, Titan is the special one, as it has a nitrogen-rich atmosphere like the Earth. It also has dry river channels which humans have observed closely during the Voyager 1 spacecraft mission.

Saturn was named after a Roman God of Agriculture. Greek mythology also talks about Saturn (Kronos) as a father of Zeus (Jupiter).

BERT: Time to move.

Jimmy: Put it on Neutral!

Olivia: In the early seventeenth century, when science was just started breathing in human society, our world was limited with

6 planets. For our ancestors, Saturn was the shore of our solar system.

Luckily, in 1781 A.D., the great astronomer, William Herschel, has discovered Uranus and enhanced our vision towards our solar system. Now we had 7 planets in our world.

Now, please set time to Uranus!

BERT: We are on our way to Uranus.

Olivia: About 19.2 AU away from the Sun, Uranus spends its life as an ice giant in the outer solar system. It is about 15 times bigger than the Earth and an average human would be weigh about a kilogram on Uranus's surface.

Like Venus, Uranus rotates east to west. Uranus rotates sideways, as its axis is tilted parallel to its orbital plane. This poor situation of Uranus may have happened due to a collision with a planet-sized object in the past.

Uranus circles the Sun in about 84 earth years. A season on Uranus is about 20 years long and this unusual orientation makes the planet experience in extreme variation in sunlight.

This ice giant has a surface temperature of 216 degrees below zero. The atmosphere contains mostly hydrogen and helium, with a touch amount of methane, a tiny bit of water, and ammonia. Methane in the atmosphere makes Uranus appear to be an aqua-blue color.

BERT: Neutral mode activated!

Jimmy: BERT! Please proceed to Neptune.

Olivia: About 30 AU away from the Sun, Neptune is so far away that it's completely invisible to the naked eyes. Like Uranus, Neptune's atmosphere is mostly made of hydrogen, helium, and methane gas. Due to extra amounts of methane and some unknown composition, it makes Neptune more vivid and brighter blue.

To understand more about Neptune, they needed to send a camera, which can fly unto there and transmit back the pictures and other close details. So, for this phenomenal long journey to Neptune, government have now decided to make two different crafts. If something happens to one, at least the other one will finish its purpose, completing the mission. In 1977, when Voyager mission had one more spacecraft as Voyager 2 for a different route. These crafts were made to travel for 1 billion years in the deep universe.

To make a sling shot, Voyager 2's closest approach to Neptune was on August 25, 1989. After 12 years of leaving the Earth, Neptune was the first approaching target for Voyager 2 craft. It passed by about 5000 kilometers above Neptune's north-pole.

Neptune is about 17 times bigger than Earth and a day is about 16 hours long. As it's far away from the Sun, Neptune has a surface temperature of about 214 degrees Celsius below zero. Neptune completes a circle around the Sun in about 165 earth years.

BERT: Neutral mode activated!

Olivia: Right after Neptune, the next orbital path is devoted for trillions of asteroids, which are circling the Sun since its birth. These asteroids are mostly made of rocks and frozen with ice, as they spend their life as orphans in the end of our solar system. We still get sunlight here, but dimmer, and not bright as Earth. These trillions of objects circle in a set path and are known as a 'Kuiper belt'.

We are almost at the end of this belt and going to find our controversial planet, 'Pluto'. It was initially found on February 18, 1930, but since then there were multiples of reasons for scientist to keep it on and off from the planetary list. Humans are just finding now that there are 3 more dwarf planets in our outer solar system who have their residence in the neighborhood of the Kuiper belt.

Sun light goes even further behind the Kuiper belt. It's like a cloud around the Sun. If we take a bulb and light it in the middle of a soccer ground, a human sitting on a bench, further away will see this as a bubble of light.

This bubble light around the Sun, is often called, Oort cloud. Human-made spacecraft (camera) Voyager1 is gone for over four decades now, but it will still take about 300 years to cross this bubble and leave our solar system.

❏

Destination G
Night Stars

Olivia: 'Twinkle-Twinkle little star,

.......Like a wonder who you are,
.......Up above the world so high,
.......Like a diamond in the sky.'

This is a beautiful night when we are seeing these stars with the help of our time machine. Humans have created multiple poems, stories, and dramas by wondering about night stars.

They have always wondered about these shiny stars and thought to be as God's place. They had joined these stars, and drew their favourite characters, and created their own figures.

Human ancestors saw all these stars as a group and named them as 'constellation' to be amazed with different, imaginative shapes. They had seen the 'Orion' constellation as a hunter, Scorpius as scorpion, Sagittarius as an archer, and Leo as a lion. They had created and shaped many more animals, heroes, and leaders to draw their memories for centuries by joining star dots.

Hindu (Vedic) scriptures describe about 27 different constellations as Nakshatras. Each Nakshatra has 4 'Padas', and they multiplied them together, to get a very special number as 108 which is the holy number even today among Hindus.

As we didn't have telescopes in this ancient time, observing stars with the naked eye, was challenging. Star observation was the major achievement for Hindus for over 1200 years on this land and created a document called 'Jyotisavedanga (Vedanga Jyotisa)' and 'Surya Siddhanta' in approximately 900 BCE.

Hindus believed, the position of the stars, planets, and Moon in the sky, affect people on Earth. The exact time when a baby is born, is used to take as a base-time to tell his future and all other milestones in his life. Hindus have created their own story with stars.

While the Aryans were practicing astronomy for a mathematical calculation of planetary motions for religious purposes, the Egyptians and Mesopotamians had also started astronomy side by side, but with a different purpose.

About 2000 BCE, Mésopotamiens had started observing the Sun and Moon more closely. Eventually, they were amazed that a big object like Moon, circles the Earth every day and that the Sun has supreme power. Humans had also learnt, it somehow affects us, here on Earth.

It was 1500 B.C.E and the monumental statues were being constructed all over Egypt. Out of these construction works; Pharaoh's daughter is princess living her life in a luxury palace with servants.

The princess was another curious soul and often observed the night stars for her fairytales. She had learnt that a few night stars are fixed and stay at the same place, each night. But, few stars often move from their normal positions.

Not just in Egypt, Sumerian (Mesopotamian) was also learning about stars and planetary motions. They had created a number system of calculation of the surrounding objects around the Earth. They simplified the task with taking the number 60 as the base digit for their calculations. Humans still use this process of calculating motions today on the clock as 360 circles for 60 minutes.

Sumerians ended their kingdom and passed on their legacy to Assyrians, followed by the Babylonians, in about 800 BCE. Modern science and western astronomy are the descendants of

Babylonian's final foundational work on astronomy. They had also got to know about the pattern of stars, planets, and the Moon's position in the sky. Harvesting was getting easier with the help of star and Moon watch.

Eventually, in about 700 BCE, the Greeks and Romans had accepted, and merged with the masterpiece of the understanding of the star system from the Babylonian's. They had joined astronomy with their god's mythology. They had never changed and kept the same name left by Sumerians and Babylonians for these shiny stars.

Same as the Hindus and Greeks, the Romans also had a connection with the stars as Gods. Zeus Greek scriptures are full of gods, stars, and constellation.

Jimmy: The only true example among humanity which lies inside the Holy Scriptures. It connects our relation to the stars.

Humans had followed stars in the past to find somebody else on our own planet. This is about 2 BCE, and the long wait for Messiah all over the world, is now completed. The Jews aren't happy with human-shaped Gods. For them, Moses, and YHWH (Yahve) is everything to them. It has been over 2000 years of Jewish religion when they have come to know that a few astronomers want to see Messiah to give him blessings.

Τοῦ δὲ Ἰησοῦ γεννηθέντος ἐν Βηθλέεμ τῆς Ἰουδαίας ἐν ἡμέραις Ἡρῴδου τοῦ βασιλέως, ἰδοὺ μάγοι ἀπὸ ἀνατολῶν παρεγένοντο εἰς Ἱεροσόλυμα λέγοντες Ποῦ ἐστιν ὁ τεχθεὶς βασιλεὺς τῶν Ἰουδαίων; εἴδομεν γὰρ αὐτοῦ τὸν ἀστέρα ἐν τῇ ἀνατολῇ καὶ ἤλθομεν προσκυνῆσαι αὐτῷ.

- (The Holy Bible, Greek scriptures, Matthew 2:1-2)

"After Jesus had been born in Bethlehem of Judea in the days of Herod, the king, look! Astrologers from the East(India) came to Jerusalem, saying: "Where is the one born king of the Jews? For we saw his star when we were in the East, and we have come to do obeisance to him."

Humans have made many relationships with stars through out the times. But to go, one step ahead and do some ground work, humans have built the most sophisticated, biggest, and advanced telescopes. Now, they can closely observe our universe with a zoomed eye.

Modern humans have also created a map of the 'Universe' and divided the entire sky in about 88 different constellations (patches). Not only the sky which is above the Earth, but even the Southern pole sky of Earth as well.

Xing: Professor! How long have these stars been shining for?

Olivia: These stars are shining since billions of years.

.........Like we humans, take birth, live our life, get old and die, fortunately or unfortunately, the stars follow the same kind of life cycle. An ordinary star usually lives, about 10 or 11 billion years and usually take birth with the same process as our Sun did, with a couple of hydrogen atoms.

A star formation, usually transpired in a colourful dust and cloud, is called, 'Nebulae'. It's impossible to estimate the numbers of nebulas, but each galaxy has over thousands of these star factories. Out of many kinds of Nebulae, one kind of nebula produces stars.

A star leaves its home in a very early age making its way out from its crib as nebula. This moment of leaving home is not worthless because it will go and shine in somebody else's world like our Sun does for us.

After leaving home, a star creates its own territory in a widely empty space. Eventually, it gets about a hundred times bigger than our own Sun to become as a 'red giant'.

When a star increases its size, other objects in the solar system burn, and engulfs into it. In this process, the outer portion of the radiative zone increases, and the core shrinks down until it runs completely out of fuel. When it happens, planets, moons, and asteroids become lost in this chaos. The core releases, generating maximum energy of its life, when a star become red giant.

After a peak, the core usually stops producing energy. The outer part increases this size, but the core starts to shrink down until it reaches the molecular level.

Once it's completely out of fuel, it blasts as a super beast as hundred billion atomic bombs together. The blast is completely magical with a mesmerizing beauty. Modern humans often call this process as 'Supernova'.

A supernova releases millions of organic-rich crucial elements and matter, which can cover-up to a few light years in diameter. Sometimes, these clouds of gas and dust from the supernova become so huge, they eventually give birth to other stars. This process repeats itself repeatedly in billions of years. In the Milky Way-sized galaxy, a star dies usually once in every 50-100 years.

This is again very important, as our kind of intelligent life cannot be possible without a supernova. The material we have inside our human body can have only one source, which is from a death of star. Until a star dies, we cannot get these organic-rich materials which can only cook in a starburst of tremendous pressure of heat and gas.

So, it's quite possible during our solar system formation, that a star died somewhere in our neighborhood.

Jimmy: Well, we don't know as we don't have any evidence for such kinds of supernovae during our star (Sun) birth.

BERT! Put it on Neutral and set the time to Arabia in thousand A.D.

BERT: Neutral mode activated!

Time: 1054 A.D.

Place: Desert of Arabia

Type: Past

Olivia: It's about 1054 A.D., and some star gazers are looking at the constellation of Taurus in the sky. They had experienced a super massive supernova remnant in the sky today. It's so bright and looks like another Moon in the neighborhood sky. Centuries later humans named this star burst as 'Crab Nebula'.

It is about 11 light years in diameter and lives very far; about 6500 light years away, from our solar system. This star burst is still growing at the rate of about 1500 kilometers per second. A Chinese astronomer had also recorded this incident in their holy books.

Jimmy: Crab pulsar lives and lies in the middle of the Nebula, as a rotating neutron star, which transmits micro pulses of gamma rays to radio waves with a spin rate of 30.2 times per second. The crab nebula was the very first astronomical object which was observed and identified with a historical supernova explosion.

Type: Neutral

Olivia: Well, this is just one part of a star's life. During their lives, stars often nurture millions of objects in the form of energy and light. These stars' light is also very crucial for human life.

Jimmy: Stars release this light as an arrow from a bow to never come back and rock somebody else's world.

Olivia: The distance between the stars are enormous. They remember the moment when they had left the nebulae in order to light somebody else's world, now this is the chance when they start releasing lights to go free and touch the boundaries of the universe.

Their light travels a long way and reaches the Earth boundaries in millions of billions of years. Even if a star had died, we wouldn't know, because the glow of that burst is still traveling towards the Earth and cannot reach the Earth until its speed of light covers the distance.

"Light" is the ultimate 'winner' among us all. Humans have tried to catch it, compete it, and fought over it but never succeeded. Light is the fastest object between us, on Earth, and in the entire universe.

Nothing can travel faster or even match the speed of light. Its photons travel in a freeway and divert if something stops it. Photons are motivated to go forwards and never look back.

Light travels around the speed of 300,000 kilometers per second and can circle the Sun 7.23 times in just one-second. Put it another way, our Moon is about 390,000 kilometers away from the Earth. So, light can travel up to the Moon and come back in a mere 2.5 seconds.

Our only star, the 'Sun', is about 85 million kilometers away from the Earth and its light reaches us in about 8.5 minutes. The Sun and Moon are just the neighbors, and their light reaches us in a few seconds and probably in a few minutes.

Humans have made only one thing which comes close to the speed of light (390000 kms per second); a bullet which could reach 4000 feet (1.25 kms) per second. Even with this extraordinary speed, light takes millions and billions of years to reach from one place to another in this vast universe.

The only traveler in this entire universe is light which travels from one corner to another in millions of years at a constant speed. Since light is the only thing traveling with this extraordinary speed, we have decided to keep 'Light speed' as a yard stick to measure distance in space on a vast scale.

Xing: Professor! But, how far away these stars are?

Olivia: 'Proxima Centauri' is the closest star to our Sun, which is about 4 light years away. If, one day, we make a shuttle which can travel at the speed of light, it would take about 4 years to get there. Other visible stars are placed in other directions of approximate 5-6 or 10 light years away from us.

It was a very special day when humans had started astronomy and we are still following their footprints.

The entire universe is filled with some kind of matter. Anything on Earth, and everything in the sky which we can see with human eyes, are just the ordinary matter. In the 21st century, humans have scanned the entire sky with the most advanced telescopes.

Humans have created a technological vision to find out the ratio of ordinary matter in the universe. It was amazing to know all these stars, planets, moons, and comets including us together, is about 4% in this packed matter-filled Universe.

In 4% ordinary matter, it has about 50% mass generating light and energy, and nurtures the other 50% mass like a child.

So, according to this 50% mass of the ordinary matter, it has 2% matter, which represents the night stars in the entire Universe. These billions of trillions of night-stars have the same structure as our own Sun and are composed with hydrogen and helium. Our own Milky Way galaxy have about 200 Billion stars, of which our Sun is one of them.

A star lets go its light as an arrow from the bow. The arrow often aims to kill someone, but a star light usually shines, and offer life on millions of billions of worlds.

When a star gazer looks at the sky, it's like he's in a time machine, looking in the past. These night stars have released light millions of years ago, of which some of them are still reaching the Earth. The further the distance, its light takes more time to reach us here, on earth.

The photons from these stars have travelled so far to touch the Earth surface. These stars are truly Gods, when they are alive, they give light and energy to its dependents, like us, and when they die, and they explode as supernova, releasing organic rich material, the common ingredients of human kind of intelligent life.

The oxygen we breathe, the carbon in our muscles, the calcium in our bones, and the iron in our blood, all of it was cooked in dragon fire of long-vanished stars. You, I, and everyone else are just made of star dust (stuff). This star stuff enriched repeatedly through succeeding generation of stars.

❏

Destination H
The Universal Law

Jimmy: What is this Universe? What is it? Are Gods alive in this universe or they were coming from a different world? Did they leave us here to die and survive on this continuously warming planet as global warming?

Olivia: When we are growing up about the age of 5 or 6, a human child has its own kind of world which can fit the entire universe at one place. Our imagination for this Universe starts with some candy bars, the latest video games, or maybe with some young lady playing around next door.

We grow gradually up and sometimes ask questions about the world, but nobody answers it. They always say, 'When you will be grown up one day, answers will come to you, naturally.'

Jimmy: Well, in the twenty-first century, we just move on and get lost in one of the sophisticated video games.

Xing: That's true!

Olivia: 'Writing' was the new evolution in order to understand the Universe and our unknown God. It was about 4000 BCE when humans have had started writing on the tablets. Initially, this writing was started with symbols and shapes. If people have any kind of idea about this universe, which their ancestors probably had received in the past, directly from a God. Now, they can carve these ideas and knowledge on a stone; again, with some 'symbols' and 'shapes'.

One thousand years have gone now, and Egyptians have started making some documents on papyrus-made sheets. These documents were supposed to keep the wrapped, dead body after its mummification as 'book of the dead'. Hundreds of books of the dead have already been excavated from pyramids and around the areas which have some attributes of cosmology.

Xing: Excuse my question, Professor! But why did Egyptians create a process for mummification? What was the need?

Olivia: Because Egyptians had believed that if one day God will appear, they need to recognize the person in the coffin and have information of person's life for resurrection.

Jimmy: Well! Humans have already claimed the throne of God and excavating mummies and reading these books of the dead to understand the dead people's knowledge about the cosmos.

Xing: Is it really human a God for which the Egyptians buried themselves? Why aren't humans making them alive? It's their responsibility to make them alive if they care about a dead man's feeling.

Olivia: Some of these documents are 72 feet long and often show symbols of the stars and the sky. There were also hundreds of letters, writing, and symbols that were carved on the walls of the biggest monumental buildings in the South (Egypt). However, a few historians believe that the idea of the Universe was actually taken from Sumerians (Mesopotamia).

Another 1500 years have gone, and the Jewish people are now experts in writing with words and broken sentences. This is an opportunity for humans, around the globe, if anyone knows anything about this universe, who can record, and present it in front of other humans.

This is 1513 BCE and Sir Moses has his reputation as God's messenger, and a great leader among Jewish, Hebrew, and Israelite societies. People have still remembered his greatest sacrifice for his palace when he was in early twenties. The Ten Commandments, as golden rules, are very important for humans at this time. They realize that God has spoken directly to him and his sayings are God's own words.

It is about 1515 BCE and the Israelites have settled back to Canaan with the help of Moses. According to the Jewish people 'YHWH'(Hebrew-Yahweh) is the only God Who exists in this universe, as He has spoken to Moses from a burning bush in the Sinai jungles.

Moses brought 'YHWH' to ordinary humans. Just before Yahweh, the Jews had a different god. Judah and eventually the Jews, were following a God called 'EI' which was a great worship inheritance from Akkadians.

Time: 1514 BCE

Speed: Light speed

Now, time is close when Moses actually wants to write something for future human generations that, 'What is this Universe all about?' Yahweh is giving him strength, clues, and a vision to see about our Universe.

It's amazing, but this is a time when the world's first religious document started to be crafted, and will continue for the next 1600 years.

It is 1514 B.C. and Moses' thinking about writing his first book of Genesis to tell people about this Universe. He is trying to understand the message from Yahweh about this earth and universe. The human understanding of the universe begins here as per the oldest written documents.

Genesis 1:1-23 (Hebrew translation)

1. In the beginning God created the heavens and the Earth.

2. Now the earth was formless and desolate, and there was

darkness upon the surface of the watery deep, and God's active force was moving about over the surface of the waters.

3.   And God said: "Let there be light." Then there was light.

4.   After that God saw that the light was good, and God began to divide the light from the darkness.

5.   God called the light Day, but the darkness He called Night. And there was evening and there was morning, a first day....23

Olivia: We have to remember one thing in that humans didn't have the telescope at this time. The vision for the creation was clear and Moses has written and completed this extraordinary document for mankind in 1513 BCE. He had covered the period from 'In the beginning' to 1657 BCE in this book.

Genesis was the first book considered to be as first book of Bible (Old Testament). The notion of cosmology included, majorly two things in this book, the 'Earth' and the 'Heaven'.

According to Moses, in this book, the Earth was created by God, as well as Adam and Eve on this planet. The other heaven part completes the entire day and night sky. This means that God lives in the sky somewhere and they had visited us in the past.

Type: Neutral

The Bible's Old Testament contains usually 2 different sayings about the universe and its creation. From the time of Moses until 500 BCE, the Earth was considered to be as a flat disc at the equator and suspended on water.

But after 500 BCE, this philosophy was majorly influenced by Greek's mythology and transformed their Biblical writings as Earth being suspended on nothing and in an empty space.

Apart from Earth, 'day sky' and the 'night sky' are still considered as to be God's place as 'Heaven'. Greek mythology (after 500 BCE - Old Testament) is often described that God came from the sky and went back in the sky.

Jimmy: Well, we don't know; How did they get to know so much about the sky with their naked eyes and no telescope? Or maybe, God visited us and gave information in the past and later, the Greeks had recorded this as a true history.

Olivia: That's true though! But Jews and Greek weren't alone in this mental cosmic race. The race of understanding the universe was started to get to know about God's place. While understanding of the universe and all of the great Biblical writers, Greek astronomers, philosophers, and prophets, often misunderstood the orbits in our solar system.

They have understood that the few stars are fixed in the sky each night, but a few other stars move on a certain degree from its axis. Biblical Greek writing also promotes the idea that, everything in this universe moves in a harmony and that the Sun, Moon, and planets move around Earth in perfect circles.

Jews and Greeks couldn't figure out that Earth is not the center, but the Sun is. Well, again, with naked eyes, observations of the universe is not less than God's will.

BERT: Professor! Time to move!

Time: 2100 BC

Place: East Asia

A few thousand miles towards the East, a group of humans are trying to settle down and create their own territory by a multiplier fertility reproduction. Competition is very tight as they are not alone on this land.

Aryans had evolved as super geniuses on northern regions of present India. They had created a complete cosmic time calculation which refers just not to an individual, but for the cosmos.

We do not know that, how exactly Hindus started astrology and cosmic time calculation, but they had created an official document as 'Vedanga Jyotisa' and 'Surya Siddhanta' after Rigveda's completion.

All Hindu holy scriptures, including Rigveda, Bhagwad Purana and particularly, Braham Purana, describes how this whole universe had been created. It says, Brahama is the only creator of this universe (Brahamanda). Like humans, Brahama's life is also for 100 years.

Xing: But Brahma is the creator, how come his life equals to humans age?

Jimmy: There's a difference kid, let the Professor explain it to you.

Olivia: This universe is also meant to be in existence through the whole life or hundred years of Brahama's life. According to the Surya Siddhanta's calculation, we are currently in the first day of the 51st year of Brahama's life.

Brahama's year (Brahama Versha) is a tiny bit different from human years and it has 360 days according to the Hindu calendar. 1 day of Brahma is called, 'Kalpa'.

Brahma just didn't create the whole universe, including the Earth, Moon, and birds, but created intelligent-like humans. Scriptures show that how 1 Kalpa is divided by 14 Manvantaras. And each Manvantara would going to be lead by a human(Manu).

Of course, out of 14 Manvantaras, we are leading as a human in 1 Manvantara. There should be a reason how Gods in India showed a purpose of life.

Actually, 1 Manvantara is divided in 71 Chaturyugas (Mahayuga) and each chaturyuga is equals to 12,000 Deva Vatsara.

A single Chaturyuga has 4 Yuga's as Satya, Treta, Dvapara, and Kali Yuga. Presently we are in 28th Mahayuga's, Kaliyug.

The duration of each Yuga is different and calculated separately:

4000 + 400 + 400 = 4,800 Deva Vatsara (Satya Yuga)
3000 + 300 + 300 = 3600 Deva Vatsara (Treta Yuga)

2000 + 200 + 200 = 2400 Deva Vatsara (Dvapara Yuga)
1000 + 100 + 100 = 1200 Deva Vatsara (Kali Yuga)

1 Deva Vatsara is equal to 360 Deva Ahoratras and each Deva Ahoratra is equal to 1 human year (Hindu calendar).

Modern humans often refer to the ice, stone, or bronze age, but Hindus creation of time division in Yuga(s) as ages was phenomenal.

This cosmic calculation and writing skills made Aryans become popular in no time in 2100 BCE. The cosmology in Hinduism (Sanatan) often refers to thousands of year-olds history, hymns, and prophecies, which are compiled in the Hindu sacred text.

This is still an unsolved mystery that, where did the Aryans come from on Northern India's landscape? They have included millions of years old history, and compiled in Hindu sacred texts, which is mostly taken place in India.

Jimmy: Let's just imagine, if the Aryans were the outsiders and migrated from somewhere else, how did they know about the history of Hindu gods?

Olivia: There is no physical evidence, which can confirm Aryans origin. But, this arises a question and demands a verdict that Aryans were possibly just evolved on Northern Indian landscape and they had never been migrated.

When the Aryans were settling down in 2100 BCE on this vast land, few groups of people were already living out here. Some of the left-over troops were from the Indus Valley Civilization.

A huge group of people had their own flag in the southern part of the Indian subcontinent at this time. These people were around for over 40,000 years. Rigveda and other Hindu scriptures often refers to them as 'Dravida'.

The Aryans had created a new India (Bharatwarsha) under one flag, which included the Indus Valley troops, as well as Dravidians.

The Aryans didn't force the Dravidians to follow the Sanatan religion but gave them a freedom to join together in the name of Brahma. Still, if you want to believe in something else, you won't be convicted as bouchard headed, like the Greek rulership.

The Dravidians had their own language even before the Aryans arrived. The Dravidians didn't have any powerful leader or government structure, but the Aryans fulfilled this need after their arrival.

The Aryans had included all these local languages and created one national language as 'Sanskrit'. The Dravidians accepted the Aryans and the reason was the same, 'God is one'.

Jimmy: Modern Hindu scholars often look for a question that it may be possible that the Dravidians had witnessed the gods and transmitted in broken language to Aryans and then they concluded them mathematically.

Olivia: Our ancestors were legends. They had created a path for mankind to follow. This follow ship was eventually called a 'religion'.

Whether Egyptians, Hindus, Greeks, or Jews, everyone has some kind of history, story, or religious value in order to connect with the cosmos.

We don't know anything about it, as to how ancient humans connected with their Gods, or when and how exactly they met with them and were able to write all those religious holy scriptures.

Humans are believing in science, saying, this is not possible without even going in space or having a supersonic, ultra HD telescopic view like we do in twenty-first century to even imagine these kind of religious stories about gods. Well, whether in the past or present, humans have always been looking for God.

We can say that different religions brought different techniques as a ritual or prayer to get to know about Gods and this universe.

As the new era began in the early nineteenth century, modern humans have started new discoveries and innovations in order to look for 'god'.

Few modern humans often ask, if, is there any God, in this universe?

If our ancestors have met them and communicated with them in the past, God cannot be invisible to us today. In all these holy books, especially in Hinduism and Greek scriptures, the Gods have given them their presence in many chapters.

Type: Neutral

Olivia: While modern humans were looking out for Gods in the sky, they have had to find out another kind of truth, that the Universe wasn't the same size in the past as today. It grew over the time and now its matter is touching the boundary line unto 13.5 billion light years away from the Big Bang center.

During the first few million years of the Universe, matter has started to coalesce into the blobs, which eventually would become clusters and super clusters of galaxies. And after, the universe will continue to grow until today after 13.5 billion years.

While modern humans are calculating equations and deciphering possible theories, they have understood that the first half of a million year of the universe was the initial creation, releasing energy and matter. This would establish a stage for future intelligent life and our understanding towards the truth. Human's wanted to know about God's will, When and how, God has cooked those materials which are inside us, yes, in human body.

Humans now know that God has made a sheet of 'cosmic fabric' which is unrolling as red carpet and expanding throughout the universe even today. The cosmic fabric has manufactured with many threads, which are crucial for the 'tree of life'. God has created some cosmic threads to sew an ultimate combination of warp and weft which has already been stretched 13.5 billion light years long.

This 'Cosmic fabric' had allowed matter objects, like galaxies and stars, to hang around with a stable vacuumed balance, and settling on a track to go further away in the future.

The newly cooked matter has now started forming baby stars and baby galaxies. Eventually, bigger, and bigger galaxies would form out of the matter from the Big Bang. Our own, Milky Way galaxy was born shortly after the Big Bang blast about 11.2 billion years ago.

The events surrounding the big bang was so dense that the cosmic fabric was completely burnt with an embossed image which we can still see and observe exactly as it happened about 13.5 billion years ago. Humans have made many sophisticated telescopes to capture, to detect, and observe the place exactly where the Big Bang took place.

Jimmy: The 'Hubble telescope' is one of them which can detect the left-over scars from the Big Bang. This is the oldest light in the Universe.

Olivia: The light we can see today is just a weak radiation and often called a 'cosmic microwave background'(CMB).

Humans usually detect CMB on Earth when microwaves carry photons with it and come to us after a phenomenal and multi-million-years journey through space.

On its cosmic journey to us, it passes through multiple galaxy clusters containing ultra-high energy-charged electrons. While it crosses out the boundary through clusters, these weaker photons often get enough boosts of energy for further travel.

It is very hard for humans to detect these boosted photons even with most sophisticated telescopes ever made by mankind. Astronomers are confident that if they can understand the fundamental properties of the 'Universe', they can make a revolutionary change and lead us to the god's place.

The Big Bang was the birth as the creation of our Universe. It blasted out super-charged particles smaller than the atoms. It has released trillions and trillions of 'matter'.

If God ever thought about creating this universe, that would be a big harvesting field with some star seeds. On a cosmic field, with some 'matter seeds' in a hope of intelligent life like us, it would harvest someday.

'Light' is out of many cosmic threads which have the supreme power, for us, let's example, is life. Without light, our kind of human life would not survive.

Light is created from the stars and shine through out in space. Millions and billions of them usually join together as a heard of sheep to form a whole galaxy which shines as a chandelier hanging on nothing, in the dark, and empty space.

To measure the distance in the deep universe, we often use different techniques in the twenty-first century. There was a technique which was evolved in the early twentieth century as 'Standard candle'. It had simplified the equation since it was easier to compare the dimmer and brighter light. After the measurement of brightness, you can exactly tell how far they are from Earth.

The other kind of technique to measure the distance to alien galaxies, humans have now decided to have a surveillance on the speed of recession of other galaxies from our galaxy. So, the speed of our neighbouring galaxies are getting away from our own because of the overall cosmic expansion.

We usually see the stars with naked eyes and often watch further galaxies with the help of modern science and technology which is telescope. When we watch them, its light travels to us, our eyes, and the Earth.

Here, we have step in the light again, as it is the only winner in the cosmos. While Sir Isaac Newton was growing up, he has just discovered that sunlight consists of multiple colours in it which we see as 'Spectrum'.

A spectrum contains multiple lights with different wavelengths in it. So far, humans have understood that sunlight is the only source of heat.

It was later found out that each colour in the spectrum carries a different amount of heat and other than blue and red, there is one more light which has the longest wave length, carrying the most heat as 'infrared'.

Like the infrared light, humans are using and have discovered many more lights. They use these lights to observe the Universe in a smarter way.

In the 21st century, modern humans have built many telescopes which are sensitive to different parts of the electro-magnetic spectrum. To observe, each wavelength in the spectrum, modern humans have created different kinds of light techniques. This is getting easier for humans to calculate distances from another object, by calculating their recession, as red and blue shifts of the spectrum of the light.

Human eyes are powerful, and can see far, distant night stars, but it is not powerful enough to look at every aspect of the universe. Everything is so far away that humans cannot see certain things with the naked eyes.

We can see the same patch of the sky with different lights and can find different answers in hidden stars, which are further away in the universe. In gamma ray light, for example, is to watch mysterious explosions in distant galaxies. Infrared light, to see the hottest place in the center of the Big Bang with microwave light, we can see all the way back to the birth of our universe.

Apart from the Egyptians, Hindus, Greeks, and Jews, the ultra-modern science created a theory as per looking at the sky with infrared light. After looking with this light, scientists summarized that initially, all the matter in the universe got together and blasted outwards, creating new matter.

The Big Bang didn't just release an ordinary matter, but also released a kind of matter which has lots of energy in it, capable enough to move even galaxies with its force. For general public understanding, scientists have divided the matter in two parts, the matter we can see, and the matter we cannot see.

The matter we see is an ordinary matter and includes you, me, everything we see on Earth, all of these night stars, galaxies; whatever we can see with our naked eyes, or with a telescope.

The other type of matter which we cannot see, is still an unsolved mystery. But equation shows its existence and that it's real.

When God was distributing power to different threads of the cosmos, Light has gotten some power, but Gravity got the supreme leadership under God's command. Gravity is another thread of the cosmos which tells the space time fabric how to curve.

It had started with a moment of Newton's life when he observed that an apple is just not falling on the ground but, two different mass objects are making attractive force to contact. The same law of rule goes with all those stars, galaxies, and supernovae.

The bounded gravity from the Sun, the force of all planets, moons, and objects, is to circle at a constant speed. If God had decided to increase this speed by less than one percent, the Earth will leave the orbit and make its way out of our solar system. The same way, if speed slows down, the Earth could end up hitting Venus or Mercury, or engulf inside the Sun.

The Big Bang blasted out energy and matter particles. Light was responsible for carrying energy from one corner to another and matter was thrown as the supreme power of gravity.

The visible or ordinary matter has mass which releases gravity in a unique proportion. But there is another kind of matter that exists which generates six times the gravity than the ordinary matter.

Xing: What kind of matter, Professor?

Olivia: 'Dark matter' is a matter which generates an ample amount of gravitational force which makes us alive.

Dark matter's gravity usually effects bigger objects, like galaxies for the smaller objects, like planets and moons, no discrepancy is found. Within the galaxy, it effects little or less. The swirling motion from the center uses its gravity generated from an ordinary matter and making stars within the galaxy cluster.

Dark matter also doesn't affect the Moon's orbit around the Earth or other planet's orbit around the Sun. Dark matter keeps the galaxy in one piece. Its gravitational force from the outer arms of stars slows down in centric gravity proportion.

The ordinary matter which we live in, is created from a nuclear fusion as star birth, and we born with it. But Dark matter doesn't interact with light and doesn't mix with nuclear fusion. It generates gravity, the same way as ordinary matter. Dark matter exerts a gravity, to which ordinary matters responds.

The Cosmic race is running at the speed of light. The fabric is stretching indefinitely with some sort of mysterious energy. This energy speeds up the space to go up to indefinite time.

And at this time, Dark matter's gravity, and ordinary matter's gravity, stand tall as tag team championship contestants against this mysterious dark energy. With two competing effects, gravity wants to make stuff stable in the same place in space, but the expansion wants to dilute it.

Dark matter made its home in between the galaxies in empty space. Space looks empty, but other than Dark matter, its home for various objects, like dwarf galaxies, orphan-less luminous stars, high energy charged particles, and some mysterious quantum energy.

Dwarf galaxies are less luminous and usually hang around the other main ordinary matter made galaxies. These galaxies are often affected by ordinary matter made from the galaxy's gravity, and Dark matter's gravity.

If they hang around too close to the main galaxy, it would be eaten and merge with it because of the powerful gravitational force.

Xing: Do we have any dwarf galaxies in our neighborhood?

Olivia: Yes, we have more than half a dozen galaxies which are close with our own galaxy, 'the Milky Way'. Our nearest dwarf galaxies are very small and often called 'Magellanic clouds'. These clouds are visible from southern part of the world.

With the X-ray and infrared sensitive telescopes, modern humans tracked down these quantum particles. Dwarf galaxies usually have a smaller number of stars, let's say, a couple of millions, instead of a main galaxy, that has in the billions.

These galaxies are hard to find and not visible to naked eyes. Particles within them are smaller than atoms. Some of them are too small to go in and out from ordinary matter to invisible (Dark) matter.

On the other side, there are other super-charged particles which live in the interstellar space. It can easily damage human life and become dangerous for us to handle. As we live in Sun's (Home star) atmosphere, it shields us from these 'cosmic rays' as ultra-charged particles.

It was a miraculous day, when Newton saw that apple falling to the ground. In early twentieth century, Albert Einstein has now decided to redo the math and present Newton's calculation of cosmos in a modern way.

Einstein proposed, that the gravity we know, works the same way it works with other objects in the Universe. He created a theory called, 'General Theory of Relativity'.

In his gravity calculations, he had to assume a hypothetical figure as 'cosmological constant'. According to this hypothesis, the universe has to be constant, instead of an expansion.

He somehow figured, that God's favorite cosmic thread as gravity, is not something which has 'supreme power', but some other kind of energy which works against it; such as a gravity which is created from the mysterious vacuum of space and works against the gravity created by ordinary and dark matter.

This negative gravity, against the matter's gravity, was recognized the same way as Einstein's cosmological constant, as 'Dark energy'. He presented a mathematical calculation of the universe (static), which represents a data that matter decides how, and how much, space would curve. And when space curves, light bends on a degree which helps in calculating distant mass objects.

Time: 9:59 PM, March 14, 1929

Place: Einstein's Villa, Switzerland

Olivia: It's a happy environment everywhere, happiness is all around, and people want to forget everything tonight and live this moment as the century's genius' birthday. Einstein was very happy, as he is the most successful scientist at this time. No one has the courage but to support his accurate, mathematical calculations.

He is having champagne with his lovely wife, Elsa, and some very close friends, including Stephen Wise, Michele Besso, and Marcel Grossmann. His PA has just whispered in his ear to come away for a second.

PA said, 'Edwin Hubble' have some convincing visible evidence that the universe is expanding, and the stationary hypothesis theory of general relativity, could not be mathematically correct.

Well, he was heartbroken, but his wife and friends were able to manage to calm him down. Yes, it was an embarrassing night for him, but he had dumped this idea as a cosmological constant by saying, 'his biggest blunder'.

Type: Neutral

Xing: Professor! So, there is no way we can possibly calculate dark energy in equations?

Olivia: Dark energy is forcing the cosmic fabric to stretch in a continuous accelerating rate at the speed of light. This fabric stretch is making our neighbor further away in another time (future). On March 15, 1929, Edwin called a press conference and stated in loud that, 'the farthest galaxies are moving away faster than the closest ones'.

The amount of matter and energy lives in the universe, is expanding and no physical rule can stop it. Objects are getting apart because of space-time stretch, our own gravity, plus Dark matter's gravity, have no part in the cosmic expansion.

It is found that dark energy holds its crown by impacting normal matter as negative gravity with 68% in the universe. The remaining 32% goes to ordinary matter and the Dark matter. Ordinary matter stays with 5% and the rest gives it to Dark matter as 27% of the gravitational force.

Dark energy is usually calculated in a mathematical term as Omega. Modern human thinks, that if you take the energy-matter density of the universe and divide it by the energy-matter destiny just required to survive, it's equal to Omega. It tells the overall shape of the universe when, energy and mass bend the space time.

According to the equation, if Omega is less than 1, the universe will expand forever in all directions, but at an accelerating rate, and actual matter and energy falls down to a critical level. If Omega is equal to 1, space will expand forever, but unto a certain line. If, let's say, Omega exceeds 1, in which space time will roll back and re-collapse back in the fireball.

Dark energy is accelerating us in the future faster than the speed of light. We don't know whether it turns out to be good thing for the future human race. The clue for dark energy could also be found in the cosmic waves. When the major objects ordinary matter act, dark energy replies as a ripple wave in space time.

❑

Destination I
The Rise of Homo Pyrus

Olivia: Time slippage is very strong, and humans are continuously failing to understand the speed of time as it goes by. Life is too short to understand about the moments; (time) one needs to live with your loved ones, holding each day as, 'precious'. A 'time recall' is the best way to understand about time's supernatural power. Out of many cosmic threads, 'time' is another kind of a thread which has some crucial effect on our Universe.

From a child to an adult, then, as an adult to an old age, it takes merely few seconds in cosmic time. The Earth itself is circling the Sun at a speed of thirty kilometres per second, and we are on it. It circles a complete orbit in about 365 days as 1 year. The Sun rules over the Earth; never stopping as does 'time'.

The ozone really makes a difference with its presence. Under this blue shield, life can slow down, allowing us to live slowly as if one wants to relax or sleep; otherwise, our home galaxy is moving at the speed of light, including the Sun and Earth. Past, present, and future would never be popular if humans didn't pay attention on time's outcome.

Like the stock market, past performances of a stock don't reflect the same value on the present or the future. Fictitious products, as a stock in the stock market fluctuates in prices, depends on the underlying asset, followed by the company's performance.

Analysis of what company we really should invest in takes us to investigate further to analyze the rate of return, for at least the last ten to fifteen years, and then we invest in the hope of capital gain (growth) on a future date. You could be lucky, if you have an opportunity to buy an Apple company's IPO, on a dollar price.

Human life is also similar to a stock market; because we carry emotions, it hurts little bit more. Human life changes in patterns, which itself exhales a style, usually led by a leader, technological change, or catastrophic chaos.

Leaders like Moses, Jesus, and Muhammad had the power to change the world and their thoughts towards 'Almighty'. They gave their presence as one human, giving other humans, a god-kind of relief.

Catastrophic chaos can be explained with the story of human life, which completely vanished chaotically about seventy-thousand years ago due to Toba volcanic eruption. The hot lava beneath the Earth's crust brought poisonous gases and carbon dioxide, which covered the atmosphere with dark smoke. The hot lava also drives methane to come out the crust, creating havoc for the next eight years with its continuous global, volcanic winter.

This situation ended almost all human life; only a few hundred, to a thousand humans, managed to survive. The northern ice cap soaked numerous amounts of oceanic water which froze up to the entire U.S. today. The global situation brought back the ice-age one more time. The land mass, previously under water, appeared to be a new gate for further, human migration.

The survival needed special techniques which made Homo sapiens, Homo Eructs and Neanderthalensis, who were to survive. Other cousins couldn't survive, but they tried hard to. We want to pray for them now, as we know they had survived before the Toba volcanic, mega eruption.

Technological change can be explained as a decision of a group of people or society to agree on something. A society is run by a government which have the majority of votes in the case of federalism.

In the early twentieth century, humans have now decided to live with minutes and hours. But, in reality, time is casting them into the future at the speed of light. Looking at the past data of human life, the stock market may help to understand our future.

The future is certain with the law of nature at certain times in the future. The Earth exists from the last 4.5 billion years, but of a single cell, and bacterial life, which evolved right after. These bacteria helped in filling oxygen in the air, building a lively atmosphere, of which we are still breathing today.

These single cell lives were evolved in a more complex life as climate changed over time. Bacteria's then, branched off in multiple different eggs of life, starting under the ocean about 4 billion years ago.

Life is around for such a long time, but we humans have got off the trees just only 300,000 years ago, which is a mere 0.004% of the Earth's entire life.

Daphne: So, why are we playing a character in the very end climax scene of this land which we call, 'Land of humans', today?

Olivia: Nature has fine-tuned itself so that intelligent life, like humans, could possibly evolve after 4 billion years of life's 'life'. The Sun is at the perfect size, and the Earth's orbit's in a habitable zone, is safe now. The Moon is at a proper distance of which humans can have a 24-hour day to live and enjoy every moment of life.

Jimmy: On a truth note, as we weren't in the past, we wouldn't be breathing in the future with the brutal climate conditions. In the past, we were fortunate that humans didn't exist and when we exited, we weren't machinelike as us today, meaning, no natural extraction, and no carbon emission.

The law of nature is that nothing is for 'ever'. Anything which has started, has to stop, or destroy one day. The cosmic calculations in the Hindu Vedic scriptures show how different Yugas (Ages) comes and goes under one Mahayuga and Manavantra.

Xing: So, this means, only 'gods' can stop this catastrophic global warming effect, as it's already out of control.

Olivia: The Hindu scriptures describe the God, (Kalki), who will give his appearance as 'God's avatar' at the end of the present age (Kali Yuga). The challenge in 'Kali Yuga' is that Kaliyuga itself is longer than the entire mankind's timeline.

The planet is warming up on a continuously gradual accelerating speed, and God will take another four hundred thousand years to be appear as Manu for this Manvantara.

At the end of the seventeenth century, many humans have starved to death. A small decision or stupidity could spoil your crops, affecting thousands of households, in the economy. Less or more rain was found as a danger for agriculture for the worst, or no production.

In between 1692 to 1700, many countries have faced major food shortages which forced many people to eat dirty-like food from waste or garbage. Yes, this doesn't sound right, but millions of people died in many countries with hunger, plagues, and other kind of diseases. At this time our medical science was not as good as it is today.

Even after this brutal chaos on Earth, the gods haven't shown up. After a long wait for the Gods, humans have now understood that the brain is the only way to fight with our bad decisions. Humans have now created their own medications, which will help them to get by with plagues and other disastrous diseases around.

BERT: Nineteenth century begins.

Olivia: Whether is so perfect right now? At this time, global warming is happening, but people just don't know yet. If anything's going to happen, who's concerned about this?

Manual drafting, writing, and proper documentations are the primary white-collar jobs in the early nineteenth century. Construction sites, especially production houses, are full of workers with humanistic muscle power and strength which has been polishing our society since mankind's integrity.

Global warming acceleration was majorly started, affecting people in the last half of the nineteenth century. The worst thing happened when humans tried to save themselves by making luxury items that can help them to survive under terrific whether conditions, such as winters and summers.

By the mid-nineteenth century, a man named, Michael Faraday, knows how 'motion' works. He had already invented an electric motor, transformer, generator, and different other kinds of machines for residents and factories. He has understood how motion generates electricity with the help of energy.

This was the greatest achievement for mankind to understand electro-magnetism to send or communicate through technology. The connection as voice chat, video chat, or text between us with the help of satellite orbiting our planet, was a great work from Michael.

Humans have now offloaded their muscle strength work, notably for mass production processes with machines. Headlines in the newspapers in the nineteenth century that, 'machines have taken over humans', are somewhat settled now. It took a while for them to understand that machines are for a good sake. They don't harm, but sit at a place, and work with a push of a button.

To run machines, humans now have to pay a huge amount in carbon emission. They needed fuel and energy to run the show as machines. God probably would not be happy to see this chaos on the planet held by Homo sapiens. They are getting smarter, but still burn coal, gas, and oil, which disqualifies them from the intelligent list in the twenty-first century.

The invention of the motor helped people make heaters, coolers, fans, and eventually air conditioners that has affected the Earth on a grander scale by emitting carbon.

This is 1925 and people are enjoying their luxury life all over the world. One man's motor invention has now widely been accepted as a part of society all over the world. Humans are setting up factories to make machines, and then sell them on a commercial basis to produce more goods and necessities for the growing human population. Now humans have a brain, powerful machines, and a fast, growing economy, but on the other side, they have a Global warming present, as a return gift.

This moment was completely magical with Rolls Royce's new Ghost Piccadilly roaster model car. Humans have never had this kind of attitude before. He seemed like an arrogant and greedy human at this time. By far, he understood that the human mind is capable of doing much more, when only one human can alone affect many lives on earth, of course, 'in a bad way'.

In 1945, a man on the American subcontinent understood the science and technology behind the Sun. Julius Robert Oppenheimer, who is a physicist, mostly spends his time in a laboratory. He is not evil, but he has an idea, that being, making a machine which can make his country stronger.

His idea of making a giant machine (hydrogen bomb) which can destroy enemies like a fly. Army officials of the U.S. army are now aware of Julius's work as the father of the atomic bomb.

This machine (atomic), releases more energy and less matter. The bomb is super-powerful and can easily damage an entire city in no time. Julius has no option but to present this evil work for his country. It was used in 1945 twice, during World War II.

Hundreds of thousands of people died because of one person's arrogance. Other than God, no human holds an authority to take another human's life. But, humans wanted to react as 'Gods'; they wanted to decide another human's life with the power of machines.

Type: Neutral

Olivia: Like software and application in computers, humans then created technology which could help motors and machines to work in a smarter way.

It was 1973 when humans made a clutch of chip boards, nuts and bolts, and called them, 'Computers'. It was later claimed that it works better than the human mind.

Of course, it does - when humans are getting busier in other complex things in their daily and personal lives. Due to multiple thought processes, humans sometimes get slower than computers. Computers happened to have a heck loaded memory capable of calculating numbers. Drafting letters and store files was a revolutionary work for mankind.

It was a great day of 1992 A.D. when humans gave this computer a new kind of soul as 'internet technology', changing everything. Manual documented stock markets have started to be in appearance to everyone from their work or homes, rather than the stocks exchange lobby.

The twenty-first century has started a new addition in computers: CD drives, flat screens, blue tooth supportive mouse's, and keyboards drawing a new line of technology.

This is 2010 and the ancient human carries a smartphone in their hands now. These are the miniature versions of the legendary big-sized computers. Smartphones carry internet technology, which uploads and downloads, multiple versions of files online.

We humans often see catastrophic change in our lives from our childhood until death. How many generations were before us? Two generations before, there were not even cell phones or computers. Without this revolutionary technological advancement, we feel meaningless today.

Olivia: By the end of the twenty-first century, humans will enter into a new electric world as Kardeshev Type I civilization. The total production, consumption, and procurement of energy, from its home star regulating from its home planet, will make humans intelligent enough to qualify under Type I program.

To become a Type I civilization, the Homo sapiens breed has already been nominated in the universal technological world. This happened on October the fourth in nineteen-fifty-seven when the Soviet Union launched a soccer-sized radio satellite into the space orbiting the Earth.

As human species rides into the future, they will offload necessary and unnecessary data from their minds to online internet technology. Online data storages would keep your personal data safe and secure. There would be multiple database companies evolving, carrying important, and secretive, data for you.

The safety of the data is crucial. This is very important that database providers are genuinely credible, and their reputations should proceed its goodwill. Google drive from Google and iCloud from Apple will start its journey as major database providers in the beginning of the twenty-first century.

The company you are using for keeping your data will also use it secretively and advise you in return, periodically. Facebook often creates a video with your memorable moments, or YouTube, which plays music you want to hear. This is what they have learned with the previous selection of music, singers, or news. It recognizes the patterns of your choices.

As homo sapiens enter into future life, they will add another biometric individual lock. Biometric locks, as touch ID and face ID, would evolve as an addition to smart devices.

Humans are highly intelligent, but not intelligent enough for this universe. In the 'race of future', machines are replacing humans on a gradual scale. Machines are getting its soul replaced every now and then with an updated technology. The transition from non-tech to a complete electric civilization, would be a continuous change as advancement and updated materials.

Humans will need more data, knowledge, and information to survive on this planet. Sapient has already been offloading their knowledge and personal information to online database. The online data regarding your personal information, such as medical history, educational, family, or work history, et cetera, may be accessible to somebody else who is waiting to advise you on your situation.

Starting from hunting and gathering, then writing, and now a complex, matrix life full of knowledge, is overwhelming. No human has time to keep all this information in their minds and survive. This habit of clearing the mind with irrelevant information, would give birth to a new kind of specie.

As technology improves, humans are lacking behind in reinventing themselves, and catching up with the technological world every little while. Technological improvement will also help machines to be compact in sizes.

Humans will reshape the same machine as new technology arrives. New technology isn't cheap either; in order to update yourself and use a brand-new technology in the market, humans will have to pay a huge amount.

Our educational authorities, starting from preschool to high school; and colleges to universities, are still talking about credentials, online learning, and some sophisticated crash courses. By the time a child procures his final graduation program, past education has already been 'outdated'.

The job he has prepared for all his life, has already been taken over by computers a couple of years ago. He feels he needs to be re-educated and contribute his share to the work force.

For an example, some older people still want to be away from technology. They say it's stupid and they like the old school idea, the way they have always lived. Older people say that they were born when there was no technology, and they will die without using it.

After a generation or two, there would be a race for human survival. This isn't going to change our continuous technological change, but society will force you to change according to the newer technology. If you don't reset yourself every five years, past technology is no good, and you will lag behind.

Technological victory was just one side of the story. Humans are actually losing its battle on the other side. In the near future, with the risen ocean level; followed by less land, its habitant will become twice the population today providing no calamity happens on our planet. This is 2030 A.D., and humans are getting irrelevant for each job.

Today, machines can do everything what humans cannot do. They can talk, sing, and even give you a solution, when you have a break-up with your girlfriend, and maybe if you are lucky, you can get a list of the next possible girlfriends who have the matching attributes to yours.

Where populations grew by 27% from 5.2 billion (1990) to 6.6 billion in 2008, their consumption level of energy has also increased significantly by 40% in 2008. Since then, the world's energy consumption has been increasing gradually as we are entering in the future for a new electric world.

Energy usage is not wrong at all, but the choice and the source of energy could possibly make an insignificant difference. As human civilization grew, it had to dig more, burning more natural resources as coal, oil, and gases from the Earth's crust.

Using these natural resources of energy was a shortcut plan for mankind. This has changed human's mind to an algorithm. As human needs are pushing them to consume increasingly more energy without using much electricity, it's making their situation worse.

Now, the real question is: are the Gods coming back to save us? Or maybe this is just a test for mankind, if our limited intelligence can grow and save ourselves from this disastrous global warming?

BERT: Approaching 2030 AD

Human consciousness is still an unsolved mystery, but in recent years, scientists have concluded that how human decision-making is enacted, has a chemical impact from its body. A pattern of selection of 'right' and 'wrong' things, suitable to you, is crucial. However, humans have a free will and they choose their answers with physical and chemical laws, which are obeyed and governed by genes, hormones, and neurones.

In 2030 A.D., Google and iCloud already have an immense personal data about you. All these years of data will be utilized in order to advise you on your future decisions just by looking up your past data, such as the stock market.

Apart from Google and Microsoft, Apple is running side by side with iCloud database. The 'Siri' in your iPhone is becoming more complex. If you say hi, she says 'hi', if you say 'directions'; it will direct you.

The creation of super-digital intelligence will open the doors for new, emerging industries. Super-digital Artificial Intelligence will give its launch as beating world champions in each category, leagues, and games, in an easier way. No human would ever challenge an AI in any championship. All they need is to read, scan, or download the rule book, and play, and beat the opponent.

A new hardcore championship in 2030 is usually arranged in between the two AI's because humans have again found a new game by watching other's fight.

The whole new purpose behind an AI technology is to completely take over a human's mental (Cognitive) work-load. Actually, Machines have done the same thing with humans (physical jobs) in the late nineteenth and twentieth century. Just because AI is billions of times ahead in cognitive intelligence, or task processing speed than the biological mind, humans will let AI make decisions for them.

They are fair and usually go by rules. Each human would have their own digital AI which can be accessed online, anywhere in the world. Your AI would also play a role as your physician. If you hold your phone or wear a smart watch, AI will scan your biometric data and tell you about your blood pressure if you are angry with this world. The data about your heart beats and the oxygen level in your body is going to safely keep, analyze, and summarize you, and the results are just a pop message away on your smart device.

The future human race would be under the command of 'artificial intelligence'. Due to advanced machines and technology, humans have minimal jobs to perform. Human's physical attribute was replaced by machines in the past, but the only remaining cognitive attribute is also taken away by artificial intelligence now. Computers are outperforming humans in remembering, analyzing, and recognizing past patterns.

In 2013, Carl Benedikt Frey, and Michael Osborne, (Oxford) published a detailed research on future human irrelevance and employment in future. Both of them created a computer algorithm that can estimate a future job probability.

With this algorithm, they have determined that by 2033 A.D., about 99% of telemarketing and insurance underwriting will be replaced by computers. Cashiers, chefs, waiters, tour guides, bankers, drivers, security guards, bartenders, and carpeting jobs will significantly drop in the near future. Some experts believe that, one day, AI will outperform humans in each category. A unique creation as an AI, Homo sapiens will never regret, as it controls the motivation of a system smarter than themselves.

Governments and corporations are building its first artificial super-intelligence now-a-days. As Homo sapiens have shaped, so called technology from 1957 with radio satellite to smart phones in 2010, AI will touch this kind of popularity in 2030 A.D.

An English pre-eminent scientist, the Late Professor, Stephen Hawking, stated that machines and technology are going to rule human society one day. He said, "The development of full artificial intelligence could spell the end of the human race."

Multi-millionaire, chief executive of Tesla & SpaceX program, Elon Musk, has also mentioned, "AI is our biggest existential threat".

Time: 2050 A.D.

Humans now have a fifty year of long relationships with Artificial Intelligence. A child to an old person, technology and being electric, is everything with a proud feeling to Mother Nature.

The continuous speedy time will cause the human race to connect even closer to AI's, rather than a handy device. Few geniuses of the century have already created human-brain and machine interface systems, which can connect the human mind to a computer device, 'wirelessly'.

There are many treatment centers which are providing you a body-built internet satellite surgery. Different chip options are available through the government and private organizations. Prices will drop as society demands this future technology widely.

Xing: Excuse me, Professor! What is the need of this technology and why are humans going to have such a kind of a chip in their heads? It would lead mankind, to which direction?

Olivia: As we have seen, that, how AI was beating the world champions (Humans) in the past. They are millions and billions of times ahead than human capabilities.

As humans have created machines, then computers, technology, and then the internet, AI would rise as the newest technology. There is no point to be dumb, if we know something; we will make it and if it is efficient more than humans, why wouldn't be a good idea to use of it?

If AI(s) are smarter than humans now, what humans are going to do? This notion of arrogance and controlling behavior will make humans experiment with their minds and connections, to the neurons, in order to control AI's from their mind.

The human brain is a three dimensional, very soft organ, which has been developing since our first mammal ancestry. Inside this soft pudding, there are billions of cells, including neurons that are constantly interacting with each other electrically, and also exchanging chemicals.

In order to make the human mind as a wireless device, they can interface, either electronically, or chemically. To be honest, it is not easy to make such a small device which can be implanted in our sensitive brain without any tissue damage.

Billions of neurons work together with rejuvenating organs, making the basic building blocks of the organism, in the human body. Voltages are controlled by concentrations of ions inside and outside of neurons. So, humans have now learnt to control the concentration of ions in order to control and connect human mind to different devices.

As bible describes, 'It puts under compulsion all people, the small and the great, the rich and the poor, the free and the slaves, that these should be marked on their right hand or on their forehead. And that nobody can buy or sell except a person, having the mark, the name of the wild beast (AI), or the number of its name. This is where it calls for wisdom: Let the one who has insight calculate the number of the wild beast, for it is a man's number, and its number is 666.' (Revelation 13:16-18)

"And I heard a loud voice out of the sanctuary say to the seven angels: 'Go and pour out the seven bowls of the anger of God on the Earth. The first one went off and poured out his bowl on the earth. And a hurtful and malignant ulcer afflicted the people who had the mark of the wild beast (AI) and who were worshipping its image'." (Revelation 16:1-2)

Type: Neutral

The Earth's magnetic field is extremely huge in comparison to humans. Humans are transparent to the magnetic field, and we don't even feel the hundreds of kilohertz frequency of amplitude.

Humans have found a new magnetic smart dust particle in the Earth's magnetic field which is crucial for mankind. The dust is made up of tiny, magnetic, amphiphilic particles that coat droplets of organic and aqueous solvents.

After a couple of processes, diluted with a fluid, it makes it ready to inject in the human brain. This particle is about one of the ten-thousandth part of a pin-point. This particle has some organic droplets. The groups of neurones surrounded by the particles will experience the heat, becoming activated, while the rest of everything stays static.

This technology will give the human mind an online access of infinite information of the past, present, and future. Humans will become super humans. They all are world champions, and AI's are now the absolute companions to lead the earthly world. With this brain-chip interface technology, humans can communicate without even opening their mouths.

Each human would have a private, as well as public data, stored online. You can leave some information open as pictures and videos for friends and public views. Public can visit your profiles through their minds and can even experience your videos if they are available.

Daphne: That's what we knew about Gods.

Xing: Yes! Only gods can talk without even opening their mouths. Only they can communicate through minds.

Jimmy: Think yourself, are we the Gods now?

Olivia: This is maybe just a human distillation of exploration. In the future, humans don't have to stick with just five senses, but they would have connectivity of hundreds of senses. For an example, infrared and UV light sensitivity.

An extension of human beings as AI's, may play a powerful role in the near future, who knows if they would actually take over humanity as per brilliant scientists of the century? Decision-making is everything, so if we pass on this job to AI's, it would literally the end of mankind.

Humans are burning, all the natural resources, such as coal, gas and oil, on a daily basis, and at the same time burning the bridge which could save them from a calamity change.

There is only one bridge which can help human race to go on the other side, but humans are burning this bridge in order to save them at first place. Humans should surely have a plan to fly over it when there is no bridge. Maybe, AI will help us to cross this bridge one day.

❑

Destination J
Godism

Olivia: When a human child is born and raised in society, he often hears that, 'God is one and he is great'. A growing child understands that God is the one who has supreme power on Earth and beyond. God doesn't live in between us, but we can connect with them through a person, prayer, or some ritual. God's are the creator, and they are the destroyers.

There are certain guidelines for 'Gods' to follow in the compliance of 'justice'. This kind of human belief often leads to an anthropomorphic cognitive approach, which determines the god's value system, and his mercifulness.

'Rewards' from God's usually come from happiness, health and peace, whereas, punishments lead to a war, major decease, illness, or natural disasters. In a nutshell, God has a very strict guideline for 'justice' and you better be following the same.

The newly born child has become a young man. He has been learning and practicing his religion and is quite happy with it. He works hard during the day for his living and spends the remainder of the time with his family.

The sooner he gets some time from his complex life, he prays to a God. A prayer, ritual, or meditation could also vary, person to person, as it depends on the kind of family you have raised.

God's also give multiples of choices for you as if you want something from God, maybe a wish, or a girlfriend, or if you have nothing in demand, you can simply make your wishes to be healthy.

After a long wait for Gods, naked sapiens have now finally decided to send radio signals through-out the solar system and space in the hope of a return-message from God or if not any extraterrestrial.

In the search of 'God', modern humans thought to be smart and found a communication technology, as radio signals transmission in space, and keep sending them throughout the cosmos, which was majorly started in the late twentieth century. Radio waves are easier to travel in free space and God might receive them from their earthly creations.

This was the obvious thing for mankind to send radio signals to contact other forms of intelligent life, like humans. Imaginations for some extraterrestrial life is not a new phenomenon, but it's been recorded throughout the religious, spiritual, and scientific past. The holy scriptures describe, how Gods have appeared from clouds, sky, and outer space.

Most of the gods later believed, that, sending radio signals in order to look for their creator, was 'revolutionary', but not enough. After a silver Jubilee of radio wave exploration for Gods, humans feel helpless today. After this failure, scientific humans might have to accept an orthodox way to reach 'god' through religion.

In a quest of 'Are we alone' in the universe, religious people's belief has somewhat damaged now, as they were hoping and waiting for Gods to come one day and give mankind, a stress-free life.

"Remember Abraham, Isaac, and Israel, your servants, to whom you swore by your own self, and said to them, 'I will multiply your offspring as the stars of heaven, and all this land that I have promised I will give to your offspring, and they shall inherit it forever.'" (Exodus 32:13)

After an unlimited amount of waiting time, intelligent humans are now thinking to build a spacecraft which will carry a message to the Gods.

Carl Sagan, a twentieth century renown astrophysicist, who has given a representation to mankind to look for Gods and extraterrestrial, in a scientific way, has now become a director of CRSR facility at Cornell University.

Time: July 1st, 1973

Place: Radio physics and Space Research Centre, NY, USA

Carl: My friends, today, I have news and a proposal to make. I want to build a spacecraft, which would be crucial for mankind, in order to look for gods. I want to assemble a spacecraft which would have the best video cameras, transmitters, tools, and most importantly, a message from Earth to the distant Gods. Maybe the Gods have forgotten about humanity and are waiting for us to send them a message first.

The message will be secure, inside 'Golden records', which would be on board a craft. Greetings in the fifty-five different languages, music, pictures, and different kinds of sounds, would possibly show diversities from Earth, if God finds it.

Pictures of animals, plants, landscapes, humans, and other forms of life are a small presentation of Earthly life in an emotional way to pursue the Gods for any kind of help. Some major information, like civilization Type, DNA, mathematics, physics, and the solar system, was also going to be mentioned in this message to the Gods. I was also thinking about putting a map of our solar system, indicating 14 gigantic pulsars, surrounded in our solar system.

How does it sound, Ladies and Gentlemen?

(And a huge clap of applause for Carl after his speech.)

Type: Neutral

Olivia: This golden record was aboard the Voyager 1 spacecraft in 1977 to travel for 1 billion years into the future. The message for the Gods is travelling about 3.6 AU per year speed, and will be passing by a distant star, Gliese 445, in the constellation of Camelopardalis in about 42,000 AD. It's a long journey, but if the Gods don't catch it at this time, the message will proceed to another destination. Who knows, maybe the Homo sapiens breed would become a Type I civilization one day and out speed this message even before the Gods get it.

Xing: May I, Professor? Sending radio signals, photos, and maps, doesn't guarantee that the Gods would ever get our message?

Olivia: That's true, but this is what humans do, when they pray to Gods. They usually have hope that the Gods will listen to their wish and fulfill them one day. Sending a physical message wasn't a naive idea, as we have been praying throughout the eons.

After all of these transformers, generators, machines, AI's, and technology, humans really want some 'personal human time' without any nuts and bolts around. They need peace and are trying to surrender themselves to hide from this trapped, complex life.

Even after this much human advancement, it's not easy to look for the Gods in person into the deep space. Everything is so far away and human (government) doesn't have enough resources for travel, either.

In the twenty-first century, humans are sometimes confused; whether they are looking for peace, or looking for God, they don't know. Elders often teach children, that, if you want peace, then you have to go God's way and only they can help you.

Looking for Gods and extraterrestrials in a scientific way wasn't the only hope for mankind. After acting as modern and advanced, humans still have the need to look for clues in the Holy Scriptures.

God's most popular name appeared as 'YHVH' about 6,828 times in the Hebrew Bible. 'Elohim' is another translation for 'mighty ones' (gods), which is appeared about 2,750 times in the Old Testament.

There are also some hierarchy and types of angels in the Old and New Testament. Like the Seraphim, 'Fiery Spirits', they are the supreme, mostly operating from a different world. Then, Cherubim, 'All knowing', Thrones', Many eyed ones', Dominions' Carry scepter and sword', Virtues' Brilliant, shining ones'.

The next in the hierarchy line are the 'Powers', who prevent fallen angels from taking over the world, and often have a close connection with the Earth and humanity. 'Principalities' are the other kind of guardian angels of cities, nations, and rulers, to help mankind. They have always protected humans in the past and paid close attention to negative powers in societies.

The Old Testament is full of prophesies. Out of 8 billion people on the Earth, some groups of people have witnessed the Gods in ancient time. They say, 'Gods' weren't from Earth, but they came from heaven, or other parts of the universe.

After a long list of Gods and their angels, a word 'KBD' (Kavod) was appeared about 376 times in the Hebrew Bible. Kavod is often known for a heavy (some object) in ancient time. The visual properties of Kavod may usually have a burning fire, cloud, smoke, or a fiery cloud.

This kavod also has a sound, which was played usually by the gods or their angels, themselves. Sometimes, they transmit their voices directly to his chosen messenger, or in the case of mass messaging, celestial announcement is God's favourite idea. Kavod often appeared from the clouds, or outer space.

'When Aaron spoke to the entire assembly of the children of Israel, they turned to the wilderness, and behold, the glory of YHVH appeared in the cloud.' - Exodus 16:10

'All the Israelites were watching when the fire and the glory (KBD) of YHVH descended upon the temple' - 2 Chronicles 7:3

'YHVH gazed out; in the pillar of fire and cloud'. Exodus 14:24

'The glory (kavod) of YHVH appeared to the entire people. A fire went forth from before YHVH'. – Leviticus 9:23-24

'The Cheruvim lifted their wings and rose up from the land and other ofanim were opposite them; and the glory (kavod) of the God of Israel was upon them from above.' Ezekiel 10:19

'Behold, the glory of God of Israel came by way of the East; the glory of YHVH entered the temple by way of the gate which opened by way of the East'. Ezekiel 42:2,4

Balaam's donkey saw YHWH's (God) angel in the road with a sword. Number 22:21-35

When Jesus went to the lofty mountain with Peter, James, and John, while they were talking, a bright cloud overshadowed them, and look! A voice out of the cloud said, 'This is my son, the beloved whom I have approved.' Matthew 17:1-9

God appeared from a cloud to Moses' tent and spoke to him face to face. Other people bowed down to the entrance of the tent. Exodus 33:9-15

Jimmy: In the past, Gods have also conceived a child from a virgin lady. Yes, I know you probably wanted to know when and where, but it's the year that you are reading this book which is equal to the exact same year when Mary gave birth to Jesus.

New Testament believers also believe that Jesus Christ was really the 'son of God'. Thousands of people have witnessed Him, just not Him, but while He performed miracles, such as resurrecting Lazarus, the brother of Marry and Martha. He has also performed multiples of other miracles to help, heal, and save people.

At this time, the Jewish society is somewhat settled, but the Romans aren't too happy with Jesus' popularity in 30 CE. The twelve apostles, and hundreds of thousands of other civilians, have experienced the 'son of God's' miraculous powers.

Time: 32 CE

Jimmy: Jesus' human-shape may have gone now, but people can still feel His presence and connection around them. At this time, writings have already been a long way as 4000 years. It has been continuously polishing and changing from symbols, to a profound writing.

Papyrus thin sheets are easily available in the market. They can also be ordered on a special term, if it's the matter of 'New Testament'. Right after Jesus' ascension to heaven, the New Testament has started for the future human race to read about the only Creator, 'YHVH'.

Type: Neutral

Olivia: Sometimes, God has also spoken through an 'angel' and a 'dream'.

'Then the angel of the true God said to me in the dream, Jacob! to which I said, 'here I am', raise your eyes, please and see that all the he-goats mating with the flock are striped, now get up, go out of this land of your birth.' - Genesis 31:11-13

On the other hand, Muslims also believe that, 'Quran' is the purest form of the revelation given by God in speaking through an angel (Gabriel) to the Prophet Muhammad. You also need to know that the 'Arabic' language is required to read the Quran, because this represents God's language, and the translation is useless.

Jimmy: Like the Hebrew Bible and the Quran, Buddhist texts also consist of the same kind of opinion. The sacred Buddhist texts majorly concluded in 'Jataka', part of the Pali canon and Buddha-Charita.

Buddhist Holy Scriptures often starts with a dream and angel that how queen Maha-Maya came to conceive Buddha in her dream.

'The four guardian angels came and lifted her up, together with her couch, and took her away to the Himalaya Mountains... Then came the wives of these guardian angels, and conducted her to Anotatta Lake, and bathed her, to remove every human stain... Not far off was Silver Hill, and in it a golden mansion. There they spread a divine couch with its head towards the East and laid her down upon it. Now the future Buddha had become a superb white elephant... He ascended Silver Hill, and... Three times he walked round his mother's couch, with his right side towards it, and striking her on her right side, he seemed to enter her womb. Then the conception took place in the midsummer festival.'

Olivia: The connection with a God, in your dream, is a common way of communication throughout the eons. Unlike dreams, people have also gotten a day vision, or revelation of a divine message.

How could Moses get a message from a burning bush and help the Israelites to get freedom? How could Muhammad get revelations in his mind to motivate and help mankind, how Buddha and his family were able to get dreams, how Hindu scriptures talk about messages and dreams? Hebrew to Greek, Romans to Hindus, each time people have gotten messages in their mind through a God.

Jimmy: There are multiples of rituals, prayers, hymns, and related gods on Earth, and humans follow them for some reason. The greatest and biggest reason is that, what are their family's favorite God? A newly born 'son' has no choice but to obey his parents and the community.

The community is run by a few wise people, and to become an active member in the community council, you may have to be 'victorious' in the voting process. The most ancient rule of the community would be applicable to everyone.

Humans sometimes feel, that, this is not right, as physical spacecraft and ancient religious scriptures don't take us anywhere. All those dreams and messages were just exclusive given by the Gods, and only to the chosen people.

A sixth-century BCE teacher, often known as Siddhartha Gautam (Buddha), was another soul who brought a new god-kind of notion, which has focused on enlightenment without a god. Buddhism was majorly emerged as a result of international refugee movement. A sizeable amount of Buddhist followers migrated and established themselves in Western Europe, North America, Australia, and other places around the globe majorly in the nineteenth and twentieth centuries.

Buddhism, 'enlightenment' without a God, was really an attracted idea for westerners in the twentieth century. During Buddha's younger age, he saw a sick man, an old man, and a dead man. These experiences made him agonize over the meaning of life, why were men born, only to suffer, grow old, and die?

The Buddhist accounts describe that, he pursued a course of meditation, fasting, yoga, and extreme self-denial. Even after sacrifices, he couldn't find any spiritual peace, or enlightenment.

Eventually, Buddha came to realize that his extreme self-denial is useless. He wants to adopt a middle way in which he would avoid the extremes of the lifestyle, meaning, if you don't have any materialistic expectations or demand, humans would never be sad.

Once he decided to find all the answers through his consciousness, he sat in mediation under a tree for seven weeks, resisting attacks and temptation from devil 'Mara'. After Buddha's meditation, he transcended all understanding (knowledge) and reached the enlightenment. Gautam has now attained an ultimate goal, nirvana, or a state of perfect peace, and enlightenment.

Time: 540 BC

Place: Region of Sakya, Nepal

Buddha: The happiness comes from its fulfillment, but on an opposite side, unfulfilled demands would lead to anxiety and unhappiness. One must avoid the course as sensual indulgence and that of asceticism to follow the middle way.

The middle way also leads to the four noble truths:
- All existence is sufferings.
- Suffering arises from desire or craving.
- Cessation of desire means the end of suffering.
- Cessation of desire is achieved by following the Eight-fold path, controlling ones conduct, thinking, and belief.

The sermon on the middle way and the four noble truths have a complete essence of enlightenment. The very last words on his deathbed, Buddha told his disciples that, 'Seek salvation alone in the truth, look not for assistance to anyone besides yourself.'

Jimmy: Learning spiritualism through Buddha's way was a revolutionary idea. He has also described, that, divine inspiration can only be claimed through the human mind and consciousness.

Type: Neutral

Olivia: While the East was indulged in Buddhism and other major religions, there was a different world on Earth, which had a completely different notion about gods. At this time, both of the gigantic American sub-continents are majorly sovereign by wild animals, moist, broadleaf forest, and some naive humans.

These naives' are completely alien to the eastern world and surviving on this land from hundreds of thousands of years. Wild animals are cruel and don't really give any chance to human to be civilized. A huge list of gigantic human's killer in the western hemisphere starts with Bison's, Caribbean ground sloths, Dire wolfs, Saber-Tooth cat, Scimitar cats, big bears, and Wooly mammoth.

Naives' on this land have a completely different kind of godly philosophy. According to them, there is no god, but a creator who created all forms of life, plants, animals, and humans. The creator is the Supreme Being and a conception of universal spiritual force.

A spiritual journey through a consciousness platform, isn't easy. It demands lot of sacrifices, time, and meditation. Like the eastern philosophy of Buddhism; ceremonies by endogenous people at Ayahuasca, and the Amazon basin, is getting popular among humanity in the late twentieth century.

This endogenous ceremony was previously closed to the general public but, today it's a place for anyone, often visited by western adventurers, philosophers, film producers, and directors for more creative ideas of the universe.

This is not an ordinary ceremony, but maybe a life-changing moment, or a meeting with God, or maybe the gain of omniscient wisdom. This ceremony is dedicated to nature, which was created by the creator during the creation period. We shall pray to be healthy as trees forever. The trees, Sun, and Moon are the grandfathers and grandmothers who holds the supreme power.

The ceremony is taking place to connect with trees and other lifeforms as part of nature. In order to complete the ceremony, members and guests shall make a big circle, and are seated facing towards the center. It's a big flex and bamboo-made tent, covering the entire ceremony under it.

During this ceremony, guests and members often served a drink. Endogenous people from Amazon have been making, and using this drink, for ceremony purposes since eons. The drink has multiples of ingredients, but the two of them, are most important ones.

The Banisteriopsis caapi plant is one, which is plentiful in the Amazonian forest. Another popular plant from the forest is Psychtria Viridis, which is also a part of the divine ingredient. Aboriginals often boil them together for hours in order to get the final drink.

Viridis mostly contains entheogenic or alkaloid dimethyltryptamine (DMT), which goes with a monoamine oxidase inhibiter to the enzyme, and activates an ultimate, spiritual experience.

Xing: Pardon me, Professor! But it is so overwhelming to have each connection from the prophecies of the Hebrew Bible to New Testament's God belief system, especially with dreams and messages. We have also gone through it with a scientific approach in order to find gods.

The Buddhist way of enlightenment, or the Endogenous people's belief in the nature of creation are unique, but would we ever find Gods for a true communication?

Olivia: The scientific, or physical approach, was a completely separate phenomena in order to look for Gods. The past interactions with God and angels, in person, through dreams, visions, or in the form of revelations, cannot be ignored, as about seventy percent of the world population believes in those dreams.

The communication process and technology used by Gods while transmitting the message into the human brain often leads to the discussion of consciousness or sub-consciousness.

So, what is consciousness? Does this time machine have a power to go into a human's experience realm? After an AI advancement, what else do Homo sapiens need to understand about god's actuality?

In order to learn about consciousness, biology, and spirituality, at the same time, humans have examined the brain waves, indicators of stress, metabolism, and the blood pressure.

These were just the baby steps to understand about psychedelics, but they may take an aggressive approach in the near future to explore consciousness. After multiples of clues from the Old Testament, the Buddhist way of enlightenment, and Endogenous people's ceremony, lead us into deeper and deeper findings of God.

Dimethyltryptamine (DMT) or a 'spirit molecule' is a simple compound which is plentiful throughout the nature. DMT has a profound effect on the human consciousness, usually producing naturally in different parts of the human body, especially in the human brain.

Like all other molecules, such as Hydrogen & Oxygen, DMT can be found anywhere in the universe. The main property of this spiritual substance is its presence in almost all forms of life-like humans, animals, plants, and isn't just limited to Earth, but these substances also present beyond the universe in Gods mind or other extraterrestrial life, if they exist.

Other than the universal presence, these particles are also connected wirelessly, and connect themselves instantly. So, if this is true, we can connect to the gods instantly, with the same technology. As we have a tiny particle in our mind and Gods do the same; positively both are connected for communication.

Jimmy: Was this the gate for all those prophesies in the Hebrew Bible? Maybe, the same technology was used by Gods when they spoke to Moses. Maybe all those angles were connected to humans through this spiritual door. The teachings of Buddha, 'enlightenment without a God' through self-consciousness could be the same way of communication process from Gods for omniscient wisdom.

In the past, few wise people have described that, the human mind and consciousness, is the place where soul lives. Because of this soul, humans call them alive, enjoy moments of life, and often pray to Gods to connect. Humans have to be positive that this soul has a permanent official chamber in the human brain.

The usual work hours for this soul is, while you are awake, all day you are busy with your routine jobs. The soul gets it power as positive or negative charges from your body. The soul's power of effect is almost constant, but sometimes fluctuates; the variation often ranges from normal to an extreme experience throughout the day.

At night time, this soul gets quiet, but activated if you are going to experience a dream that night. This experience of connection to God also occurs near death or during the death experience. This is the time when the soul leaves the body, and right after, biology stops working. This soul sits quiet in its official chamber and also experiences your external life moments.

The moments are crucial for the soul to determine your reward as 'right or wrong', 'truth or fake', or some et cetera parameters. The soul can easily be manipulated with sound waves; for instance, if you are talking to someone, or listening to a music. Different kinds of sounds and music affects the soul of our mind.

The ancient hymns from Hindu scriptures, prayers, rituals, meditation, and yoga were evolved as one way of communication to our own consciousness, and then it would transmit to the Gods. It looked possible that the soul mediated the subjective elements of non-psychotic, non-drug induced altered states, such as dream sleep, and the effects of fasting and prayer.

Time: 10,000 BC

Place: Pineal Gland, Human brain

Jimmy: The pineal gland is a tiny organ which has its place, deep inside the recess of the human brain. It's a very small organ and often affects human consciousness, visual, and auditory pathways.

This organ also releases secretions into the cerebrospinal fluid that continuously bathes human brain. The pineal gland (PG) also nurtures the precursors and enzymes necessary for the synthesis to go to the endogenous psychedelics, such as 5-methoxy-DMT and DMT. PG also produces melatonin which is crucial for human sleep, but it has nothing to do with psychedelic experiences or connection with Gods.

DMT often contains of numerous biological modifications of dietary tryptophan. Other than DMT, tryptophan also synthesizes with melatonin and serotonin, which are building blocks for amino acid. This is very important to synthesis one of the other's as glucose, amino acid, and protein sync for proper, brain functioning. DMT plays a crucial role in regulating the human mind in a concise way.

The physiological effects of DMT usually consist of robust increases in blood levels of beta-endorphin, cortisol, prolactin, vasopressin, and adrenocorticotrophic hormone (ACTH).

Once you may connect with Gods through this technology, you will have more problem-solving abilities, and be more creative, possessing greater altruism, and less fear of death.

Spiritual experiences often lead to a metaphysical process, which takes place at a level to be objectively invisible, but the effects are subjectively visible. In the opposite way, serotonin effects are objectively measurable, but not subjective.

So, the real question is, why is this tiny organ, known as the 'pineal gland', configured in our brain, which provides a connection to the god? Gods have communicated with humans through his brain as messages, dreams, and visionary angels, and used the brain organ as a physical agent of communication.

The pineal gland releases insignificant amounts of DMT, which makes humans experience a spiritual world. This DMT hormone facilitates the soul to sneak-in and sneak-out from the body from the official brain chamber.

It's a common molecular language which connects all kinds of life together from all over the universe, and not just humans, but plants and animals feel these unimaginable experiences as well.

❏

Final Destination
2150 AD

BERT: We are probably mentally prepared for this future journey now. What would it be looking like? Looking at past data, such as the stock market, and predicting a future outcome for mankind, is crucial.

Jimmy: Prophecies in the Holy Bible were prophesied for a 'divine purpose'. The Biblical authors have documented each prophesy because they felt, that gods, (or angels), have spoken to them for a divine 'message'. Due to extremely far distances in space, maybe the Gods just decided to give mankind messages through dreams or vision.

In the future, major geological crisis, such as 'global warming', would not be the only cause for continuously changing human lives. But, as mankind follows technological advancement, effects are going to be personal and more practical. Family members and close friend circles would be going to be the only hope for help, in the case of emergency.

Olivia: As the Hindu Holy Scriptures describes, about God's 10th avatar would reach Earth at the end of the present age (Kali Yuga). The present Yuga (Kali Yuga) is the end Yuga of the present cycle of Mahayuga.

शम्भल ग्राम मुख्यस्य ब्राह्मणस्य महात्मनः।
भवने विष्णुयशसः कल्किः प्रादुर्भविष्यति॥

At the village of Shambhal, principally of great soul of brahmins, in the home of Vishnu worthy, Kalki will arive. (Bhagwad Purana 12:2-18)

द्वादश्यां शुक्ल-पक्षस्य माधवे मासि माधवम्।
जातं ददृशतुः पुत्रं पितरौ हृष्ट-मानसौ।।

Twenlwth Moon of the Madhwa Chaitra (March/April), first month of Vikrami lunar year, lord Vishnu (Kalki) will arrive, parents will mentally be overjoyed with their new born son. (Kalki Purana 1:2-15)

Olivia: According to the Hindu cosmic calculations, (Surya-Siddhanta), Kaliyuga is about 4,32,000 human-years long, which has started its journey in 3100-3200 BCE when Sri Krishna (9th Avatar) ascended to heaven.

'Kali' is a Sanskrit word and it means, black or dark. Hugely immense Hindu scholars, and a large team of scientists are connecting this word with 'dark matter' and 'dark energy', or some negative power around the globe. But it might be possible that, Gods meant 'kali' to be 'carbon'. Lord Krishna ascended to heaven in 3102 BC, and the Earth was majorly affected with global warming right after.

In the Holy books, it has explained how this world is going to be filled with happiness and joy. Kingdoms of Satan and evil powers would end just by the Lord's presence. But the long wait, for over four hundred thousand years, is very much far away. With the present resources and government funding, it is very hard to find and actually call out for Gods in person in this vast space.

In the recent years, astronomers, (Kepler spacecraft), have found that almost each night star has one or possibly 2 Earth-like planets which are orbiting its home star. The Kepler telescope is a supersonic ultra HD telescope which is only dedicated to looking for other Earths (God's place/heaven) in other solar systems.

Kepler captures millions of stars in multiples of frames per second. In order to look for the Earth like planet where humans could possibly migrate one day, Kepler is a special artifact manufactured by mankind.

Kepler captures the dim, in the light, when an object passes its home star during its orbital motion. After analysis of many orbits and study of stars, humans have found that about each star has as many as seven or eight planets. The concept of eight planets of our 'own' solar system seems to be outdated now.

There are 2 billion stars just in our home galaxy, if each star has one or two Earth-like planets in habitable zones, there would be 3 or 4 billion possible Earths just in the 'Milky way' galaxy. Looking for god's place, is now getting difficult for mankind; but also, the blink of a possibility for men's future migration.

Modern humans are tough but delicate at the same time. The human body has evolved after 4 billion years of life's life, and right now, the earthly environment is perfect for human-like intelligent life. All these planets in the habitable zone don't guarantee us, that, if we could possibly go there and start a new life one day. The atmosphere should be perfect on one of these planets to live freely, as we had experienced in sixteenth century on the American subcontinent during a huge, multinational migration.

Before you start your trajectory, to one of your neighboring star for migration, humans would have to make sure that the atmospheric composition of the planet is suitable for any kind of life. Like our atmosphere is filled mostly with Nitrogen and then oxygen, planets with similar attributes could possibly be the next homes.

It is not easy for mankind to analyze the atmospheric composition of these distant objects, and these planets are very small to observe, and often faint in the glare of the home star.

In order to look at them closely and capture digital images for details, humans need an updated telescope (technology).

BERT: Power on.

Time: October 26th, 2019

Place: 150 million miles away from Earth's orbit

Jimmy: While global warming continues, in October 2019, humans from the Canadian Space Agency, European Space Agency, and NASA, have made a phenomenal masterpiece as the James Webb Spacecraft.

JWST is a latest modern telescope which can see beyond our universe. The purpose of this telescope is not limited, but to study the first luminous glows at the place where the Big Bang happened.

This ultra HD telescope is loaded with cameras, spectrometers, and detectors to catch and record extremely faint signals. Programmable micro-shutters and infrared technology would reveal the secret of life as to observe the formation of the first galaxies, stars, and the solar system.

A technology added by ESA, is often called MIRI, (Mid-Infrared Instrument), which could separate planetary light into multiples of wavelengths on the spectrum stage. This technology consists of a camera and spectrograph which observes light in the mid-infrared region of the electromagnetic spectrum, and wavelengths that are longer than what the human eyes can see.

At this point, humans don't have any vehicle to actually get to these distant worlds, but they can capture digital pictures of these planets with the determination of atmospheric composition. Well, humans have enough going at this time on planet Earth, and 'migrating to other planets' is an idea that should go to the back burner at this time. People feel still safe and secure as per current global situation.

Type: Neutral

Olivia: Twenty-first century would involve humans in new kind of 'digital-technological' world which made its accomplishment by ancient old school computers to mini-microchip in your smart phone device.

As the Arctic and Greenland's ice are melting, risen ocean levels and less land mass are alarming red in order to back up a little in the middle of the landmass. Extra water in the ocean makes the atmosphere more humid, and not suitable for most of the major crop productions.

Sustainable production of consumable energy is in demand and very widespread in 2050 A.D. The addition in machines as technology, is gradually making them automated, with the help of AI.

In 2050 A.D., governments are gradually conquering everything which is fuel-based, (coal, gas, and oil), and turning those products into electrical. Taxi drivers, bus drivers, pizza delivery and truck drivers, would be the first to lose their jobs. It was reported by 'Forbes' that each year there were about 10 million accidents taking place, due to human error, all over the world.

Humans are not perfect, as they text and drive, call and drive, drink, and drive. In the worst-case scenario, maybe they are sleepy while they are driving, and one could possibly lose his life in a split-second. Automation in driving would provide a new line of advancement to the sapiens species if they want to go to point A to point B, safely. There would still be couple of accident occurrences with automation, but it's kind of negligible in number, and definitely not in millions.

People would understand that driving a vehicle, has about 300-400 tasks per second, and AI's can definitely drive millions of times better than humans because they don't drink, sleep, or text. AIs do not need any break while they drive and can drive for longer hours with the package of efficiency and safety. At this point, nobody, including governments, private, or public-sector companies, or any individual, wouldn't be hiring drivers at all since driving is now all automated with a GPS programs.

Other than driving, a 'health industry' would also get an irreversible hit from AI. All these years of your immense bio-metric data with the permanent waterproof watch on your wrist, (collected by google and apple), are indicating a time to pay off as your personal physician.

Past data of your heart rate, blood pressure, and sugar level would help AI to structure a complete picture of your health. If things are minor, then it can be delayed for later assistance, but in the case of heart attack, AI would call 911, as well as an ambulance for you. Things will definitely not be going to change even if you get to an actual hospital.

Doctors, nurses, and testing specialists would all drastically lose their jobs in this future technological world. Patients will be taken to a wardroom to have the remaining checkups for the cause of illness. New AI doctors and nurses would download your updated biometric data from your watch to majorly look for an actual cause of illness within the past 24 hours.

As billions of times more cognitive decision-making power, 'AI-doctors' are able to scan your entire body with a couple of electrodes, and can easily find any major, or minor short circuits in your body within a few minutes. Brain-interface chip technology would be revolutionary, as humans will be connected to the internet and online data. With the fastest growth in neuroscience technologies, AI-doctors are able to cure major diseases like cancer, paralysis attack, heart deceases, and neural problems, and give you specific medicine accordingly.

If you want to go like an old-school way by going to your human physician (family doctor) for checkups, no problem. Human doctors are capable of observing your facial expressions and some basic checkups during your visit but would still be unable to go into your bloodstreams as AI does. AI will give you an improved picture of your health right away. Everybody also needs to get helped, as soon as the decease has been identified, and going to your actual physician wouldn't be a good idea.

Each human has a personal AI and it has an extension compatible with your smart wrist watch to inform you in the very first minute of when cancer hits your lethal body.

Xing: This means humans wouldn't have to wait for cancer to be identified at first place and then a late curing procedure may take the situation out of control.

Olivia: Cancer is one of an extreme kind of disease; normal prescriptions like fever, headache, body-ache, or blood-sugar level, will not be necessary after a continuous touch of your nervous system with an AI. Doctors have known to be as God's second face throughout humanity as they cure your sin in a chemist way. Now, when the AIs have outperformed human doctors, they'll be called as a new species of an immortal homo sapiens breed. A healthy countryman could possibly contribute his expertise to his home country for a better economic development.

This change in health industry will be revolutionary, and humans will be healthy, and may maintain human life up to 150 years. This is what is written in the Holy Scriptures to you to look at:

"The righteous will possess the Earth, and they will live forever on it." (Psalm 37:29)

"Look! The tent of God is with mankind, and he will reside with them, and they will be his people. And God himself will be with them; and he will wipe out every tear from your eyes, and death will be no more, neither will mourning nor outcry nor pain be anymore. The former things have passed away." (Revelation 21:3-4)

Unprecedented advancement in neuroscience and health industries by artificial intelligence would never be forgotten. In 2050, major 'health-industry' jobs are taken over by AIs, and at the same time, educational institutions are facing major breakdowns as well. 'Professors and 'teachers', who are another face of gods on Earth and amongst humanity, would going to lose their professions permanently.

After a brain-chip interface technology, a child doesn't need any teacher to be taught as to become one of the geniuses, out of hundred students. Each human is connected to online access and to unlimited data, wirelessly accessible through mind chip. Each human is now a 'superhuman' and omniscient as to become an immortal being.

Banker's position in banking industries and a broker in stock markets are pretty much based on past data and algorithm. AI would have more knowledge about volatility than a stock agent, and most importantly, without any management fees.

Daphne: So, if AIs are taking over most of the jobs, in that case, what would humans have left to do?

Olivia: Yes, humans wouldn't have much to do in the second quarter of the twenty-first century. Complete automation and AI systems are not just making individual's useless, but governments have very little to do within the basic social justice and procurement of life. National security, national Finance regulation, and gigantic construction sites are going to be the major federal projects.

Not just one country, but each country around the globe has been going through with this major construction phase in the twenty-first century. These mega 'Worldwide construction' and sophisticated infrastructure sites, were never seen before by mankind. Giving up on very limited resources as coal, gas, oil, and rebuilding the cities is quest, to become a smart civilization.

Rebuilding the complete infrastructure would be hard for congested cities in India, China, and other major part of the world. To become an electric civilization and use direct solar energy, buildings will be covered with permanent solar panels in most of the cases.

These solar panels will provide you with electricity during the day time and would also save it for the night cycle. There are some extra systems for energy procurement, in the case of cloudy or rainy days and will be explained to the residents as soon as they enter the house.

Jimmy: Again, this is all happening because humans want to reduce its drastic carbon emission, which is making the Arctic ice cap melt.

Olivia: That's right, but before making solar power compatible to residential houses and building blocks on the ground, the government needs to come up with a blueprint of underground tunnels and transportation systems, with almost no carbon emission.

These tunnels are getting constructed all over the world for transportation, and to fight with the global warming effect, to buy some time to live on Earth. These construction sites are probably the last construction sites made by man's muscles. By this time, mostly AIs are still in digital form, but eventually they will come out of its digital soul and get an actual body (avatar) to work.

Underground construction for transportation isn't easy and often turns deadly in the case of disrupted thousands of tons of rock that has fallen on to the tunnel. With some robotic help, humans are working under the command of an anarchist government to build a more sophisticated, and advanced tunnel system on Earth.

There are majorly three lanes in the system, where the first lane is dedicated to the public transportation, such as electric self-driven trains or cars. The second lane is dedicated for emergency vehicles like ambulances, fire buses, or school buses. The third lane is for your personal vehicle to go from point A to point B as per your suitable time and convenience.

The making of these new homes is not for fun. It does not mean that AIs have taken over all of the human's jobs and they have nothing to do, that is why, they are making homes and tunnels, but this construction would be the last ace and required task for mankind to save humanity on this planet.

Type: Neutral

Olivia: As soon as the third quarter of the twenty-first century approaches, Homo sapience breeds are feeling happy and proud to be fully electric species and contenders for the Type I civilization. While many people were involved in this worldwide mega construction series, some humans were thinking differently.

As governments are building these monster ground and underground megastructures, the ozone is again affected by major heat and dust pollution. Agriculture is somewhat coming out to be thirty percent lesser this year, as per terrific global climate in 2075 A.D.

There is less ice remaining on the Arctic at this time. The excess water in the ocean is signaling a red alert for major coastal cities, like the state of California, New York City, Italy, Mumbai, and all other smaller islands, around the world.

Election is around; and the majority of people think that building gigantic tunnels and solar powered houses are not enough to save humanity. They say, that, the Earth is going down anyway, whether or not you make tunnels or premium houses.

Humans with this philosophy, often take them to the notion where some humans should go off the planet Earth as to save sapiens species. While megastructures were being made, scientists and astronomers have prepared a complete 'master plan' to settle humans elsewhere in the solar system and other parts of the universe.

The plan has been presented, in two different 'stages' in the constitutional assembly. Stage I consists of human 'migration to Mars', as it's the closest object where humans have found almost all necessary elements, which is required, and crucial for human life. Stage II would involve the settlement outside of our solar system.

During the birth of our solar system, dust, and debris around the sun created all these planets. Mars was formed almost at the same time and composed of almost the same material as the

Earth. Samples and the lab reports tell us that Earth and Mars have been exchanging rocks since billions of years. It's quite possible that life on Earth was migrated from Mars billions of years ago when it was alive.

Xing: 'Alive'?

Olivia: About two billion years ago, Mars had a thick ocean layer and a decent ozone. As Mars doesn't have enough magnetic field like the Earth, heat from the core couldn't do much but to deepfreeze the entire planet in super cold, empty space.

Right now, all of this oceanic water on Mars is frozen under the surface, and a very thin layer of ozone exists. The atmosphere is mostly filled with carbon-dioxide, and air is definitely not breathable for human life.

It was year of 2030 when the 'World Mars Oriental Society' was inaugurated in Ottawa, Canada and the deed was signed by over 70 countries in order to support and participate in the future human settlement to Mars.

The plan is pretty straight forward as to set up some artificial carbon emitting factories, which can warm up the planet and ice to be melted in liquid form, and evaporating oxygen to the atmosphere. In order to start a plant and bacterial life on a Martian surface, people on Martian ground would take thousands of years in the near future. It will be a gradual Terraformation by living on the Martian ground.

As humans do not have any experience in settling other than the Earthly continents, our neighbor, Mars, could be the first place to practice human settlement before they start elsewhere in the universe.

It is 2075 A.D., and about a 'hundred thousand' people have successfully migrated to the Martian land so far. Cargo ships are taking readymade smaller, bigger, and gigantic air-compressed domes to be assembled on the Martian ground by AIs and human labor, to make bigger and bigger human civilizations.

Mars is about 1.5 AU away from the Sun and by going there, humans will definitely buy some time for its survival. But it is still in our solar system, and an unstable solar storm or entrance of a neutron star, could end life on Earth and Mars together.

Jupiter also holds a huge gravity to keep trillions of asteroids in the asteroid belt, which is in between Mars and Jupiter. If periodic storms could unstable Jupiter one day, all these asteroids fall in the solar system. As one of these asteroids, ended life of 170-million-year kingdom of dinosaurs, it could end again. So, it becomes very important for humans to look for a condominium in another solar system where the home star is more stable and younger than ours.

Type: Neutral

While Martians are spending their life in peace and happiness with little or no effort, humans on Earth are preparing for World War III. The situation is brutal and most of the countries are facing major food and water shortages.

As per technological advancement, by far, almost everything is automated, and a handful of government officials are controlling all these financial algorithms to rule the country. A big chunk of tax money is being used, and spending by government agents on unspecified space programs, without any civilian's concern.

As per stage II, settlements outside of our solar system is declared to be as 'The World Spaceship Program' (WSP). In 2045 A.D., there was another deed, signed by over 90 countries with the collaboration of the 'World Space Association' to leave our solar system.

Time: July 11, 2075

Place: Canadian Space Centre

Today is the day when conservatives have announced a launch of unmanned probes to the different planets. Under the WSP program, the target is to settle humans in other solar systems to save humanity if anything happens to our Sun.

Kepler's initial findings of the planets was crucial. The masterpiece, as JWST, has also helped mankind to capture closer and clearer images. Infrared technology in this telescope has also helped people to understand the atmospheric composition of the Earth-like planets.

But, to go to one of these planets, is 'risky'. Digital pictures show how these distant planets look exactly like Earth. The atmospheric composition is also very similar to Earth's. A journey to one of these planets, in the hope of a new life, could turn out to be devastating. Who lives down there; nobody knows. Is there even, at least, plant life existing; pictures and infrared sensors wouldn't be enough to think about a journey.

As humans would enter in the fourth quarter of the twenty-first century, they have created another masterpiece, as a space probe named as a 'Shooting Star'.

A 'Shooting Star' is a low-cost probe attached with a micro-digital camera and few sensors as an additional requirement. It's a square shaped, paper thin, sail which has a laser propelled technology in order to complete the journey. The government has a plan to shoot as many as five thousand sails per year basis in order to look for the next Earth.

The probe will start its phenomenal journey and make separate destinations to different planets circling different stars. Some of the probes would approach their journey sooner than those who have a longer route. As low as 10 years, to thousands of years longer, a journey would be in the fate of these probes.

At the time, when the probe approaches the target planet, it will go into its orbit and capture very close-up images, and then be transmitted back to Earth. Once the probe has identified all atmospheric composition from outside, it will fall onto the planet for ground level research. With this data, humans then finally make some plans to settle on one of these distant Earths.

Type: Neutral

Olivia: In a quest to look for God's place and at the same time to secure humanity, is a long shot for the homo sapiens species. As per Hindu holy scriptures, they describe the length of the Kali Yuga as 4,32,000 years, which could be a distance in light years. Maybe it's a clue what the gods have left to humanity to figure out the distance unto the 'Heavens'.

432K light years may be a two-way distance from where 'Dashavatar Kali' is going to appear. Earth's neighboring galaxy, 'Andromeda', is about 2.5 million light years away from the Earth, so a '216K light years' distance, is somewhere nearby in our home galaxy.

Even this close distance, humans would take hundreds of thousands of years, of course, with light speed. The Gods probably would have space-vehicles, which could possibly travel more than the speed of light when we were just getting off the trees about 300k years ago.

In the range of 216K light-year diameters, there are thousands of stars and each star shows a possible Earth like planet. To figure out 'life and civilization' on these planets isn't easy even for twenty-second century humans. For now, they have to put this idea on hold and look for a place where humans can migrate in the near future.

In the radius of 12 light years from the Sun, there are about twenty-six closer stars. Right next door to our solar system, there is the triple-star system, consisting of Alpha Centauri A, Alpha Centauri B, and Proxima Centauri in the patch of the Centaurus constellation about 4.37 light years away.

Alpha Centauri 'A' and 'B' are much closer by as Saturn is to Sun and orbit each other with a tremendous gravitational field. There is a planet which orbits these binary stars, but it's too risky to live by orbiting 'two' stars simultaneously.

Proxima Centauri is a little bit further away and orbits these 2 stars from a distance of .2 light years. It's a dimmer red dwarf star which is good for intelligent life, like humans. A planet orbiting Proxima Centauri is often known as 'Proxima B', and best conjecture for humans to migrate so far.

Laser propelled sails have reached to 'Proxima B' now and transmitted back a 'promising data of life' to earthly brotherhood. But humans on Earth are asking for more options in order to migrate.

In the constellation of 'Aquarius' of about 40 light years away, another smaller 'red dwarf star' is located, often called the 'Trappist 1 solar system'. This star has a slightly bigger size than Jupiter and ultra-cool temperature for possible human migration. The Trappist 1 system consists of about seven planets, which are orbiting its home star.

Out of seven planets, there are three planets which have the same mass as Earth and orbits its home star in the habitable zone. This means that, all of these three planets have liquid water on its surface. After looking at these planets through JWST, it confirms a possible heavenly kingdom for future, human settlement. Instead of going to 'Proxima B', which is about 4.2 Light years away, humans feel that the 'Trappist' system is a better option.

Time: 2150 AD

Place: Earth

BERT: APPROACHING FUTURE!

Olivia: People on Earth are still happy and somewhat surviving on this planet. At present, there is no Arctic or any of Greenland's ice left, which melted completely about 20 years ago. There is only about 20% of land mass that has already gone under water, losing many coastal cities in this chaos. People have no jobs, and food and water shortages are getting to be bigger problems for mankind.

Almost twice the population and less land would give birth to a new political divide due to globalization and a World Spaceship Program. However, the first stage of mega construction has still been running with sophisticated tunnel systems and solar powered ground construction.

Today, a major conflict in between the civilians and the government is about federal taxation. Under WSP, the government wants a major cut in taxes from the civilians earned incomes all over the world.

At this time, under the tight political, geological, and atmospherically change, that would make people think about leaving the Earth one day. In the election campaign, leaders have a main agenda and focus on building a spaceship in order to save humanity.

Spaceship building isn't easy, but humans have experienced a few smaller spaceships making on the ground and rehearsed in the space with some minor failure percentage. A phenomenon shows that a spaceship is usually the masterpiece of the civilization it's made by.

Right now, all ninety participating countries are ready to build this unprecedented masterpiece so that humans could possibly leave our solar system one day. Each country has its equal share and responsibility in making this spaceship. About 45,000 passengers containing this voyage would take humans to the Trappist 1 solar system in about 20 years.

It is also not easy to make this kind of gigantic spaceship on Earth's ground and later lift it with the help of rockets as technically, it is not feasible, and governments have decided to make spaceships in space only. It is also not safe to build this spaceship anywhere around the Earth's orbit. If something unfortunate happens and the spaceship hits the Earth's surface, entire humanity could end up spontaneously.

After so many conferences and government meetings, the WSA has decided to build it on the Moon's surface as Moon is nearby, and with negligible gravity, the spaceship wouldn't cost much too launch in space. Each country has set up one or more facilities in their countries following the master blueprint to make spear parts, which would be assembled perfectly in the spaceship.

The World Space Association is playing a major role, as this kind of huge project needs an ultimate leadership chosen by

The Time Machine : Homo Sapiens Version

mankind. Space ship construction is going through with its first phase all over the world and would take approximately 30 years with the human-AI collaboration.

It's wonderful to say that the naked humans who had migrated from trees to land are now ready to leave the Earth by the end of the twenty-second century in order to save the same homo sapiens breed.

The future is uncertain, but the close predictions with clues and data from the past, may help mankind to understand the near future, and they can quickly re-invent them with the current technology, and jump into the competition of the future human race. The Proxima and Trappist solar systems are just the beginning of the extended human civilization, but eventually with the need of nature, humans will spread to many other star systems to inhabitant as Type III galactic civilization.

It's quite possible that by this time intelligent humans could possibly find the Gods place and invite them in person for the 'biggest holy grail supper' in the universe. But, if not, each humanity from each star system from the entire Milky Way galaxy would come back on Earth for a feast to welcome God's 'Dashawatar Kali', (10th Avatar), at the end of Kali Yuga.

"From ages past when life began
The Earth in beauty, rich and grand.
Divine appointment; breath of life;
God's Plan in Eve became my wife!

"The human race through us lives on;
Aspired faith acclaimed within the dawn.
No greater Plan than this could be;
The wonders of life's gift so free!"

– EG & MS

❑❑❑